W. Pakenham Walsh

Modern Heroes of the Mission Field

W. Pakenham Walsh

Modern Heroes of the Mission Field

ISBN/EAN: 9783337195304

Printed in Europe, USA, Canada, Australia, Japan

Cover: Foto ©Raphael Reischuk / pixelio.de

More available books at **www.hansebooks.com**

MODERN HEROES OF THE MISSION FIELD.

MODERN HEROES

OF THE

MISSION FIELD.

BY THE RIGHT REV.

W. PAKENHAM WALSH, D.D.,

Bishop of Ossory, Ferns and Leighlin,

AUTHOR OF "HEROES OF THE MISSION FIELD," "THE MOABITE STONE," ETC.

New York:

T. WHITTAKER, 2, BIBLE HOUSE.

MDCCCLXXXII.

TO

THE YOUNG MEN

OF OUR DAY AND GENERATION, AND

MORE ESPECIALLY

TO THE STUDENTS

OF OUR UNIVERSITIES,

THIS VOLUME

IS AFFECTIONATELY INSCRIBED.

PREFACE.

In acceding to the wish that I should
continue my sketches of missionary heroes,
and bring down the history of missionary
enterprise to our own day, I have prescribed
to myself the same rule which guided me
in the former series*—namely, that the
characters chosen should be those not only
of typical men, but representative, as far as
possible, of different fields of labour, and
various modes of action. The theme has

* Published in the *Clergyman's Magazine* for 1878,
and also separately as a volume by Messrs. Hodder and
Stoughton, Paternoster Row, London; and Whittaker,
Bible House, New York. The present sketches were
originally printed in the same Magazine, 1881.

with a time when the "messengers of the Churches" were sneered at as "consecrated cobblers," they carry us on to our own happier days, when their names find grateful record in royal speeches, and their remains find honourable repose in our national sanctuaries; they show us how all sorts of culture, linguistic, medical, and scientific, are being made subservient to the spread of the gospel of Christ; they prove that the age of chivalry is not past, and that the spirit of martyrdom is not extinct in the Church of God; and they bear testimony that the Gospel has lost neither its vitality nor its power, inasmuch as amongst all races, whether savage or civilized, it has achieved, and is still achieving, triumphs which may well compare with those of apostolic times.

We may challenge the history of the world to produce instances of heroism more exalted or more heart-stirring than those which are enumerated here; and we may claim for these champions of the Cross a valour and a self-devotion as disinterested as they were sublime.   Let it be remembered, moreover, that they are but examples chosen from a countless host of brave and noble men, "of whom the world was not worthy,"—men who were content to labour on in silence and obscurity, without any hope of earthly recompense, and many of whom laid down their lives in the cause of Him whom they loved and served.

These records prove, moreover, that with regard to the heroism of missionary enterprise, no body of Christians can lay claim to a monopoly. We have, and we strongly hold, our ecclesiastical preferences and convictions; but heroism like this is the outcome of Christianity itself, and it furnishes undeniable evidence that, amidst many unhappy differences, there exists amongst Christian people a grand under-lying agreement both as to faith and duty. To quote the words of one* of whom any Church or nation might be proud:—" The spirit of missions is the spirit of our Master; the very genius of true religion. A diffusive philanthropy is Christianity itself. It requires perpetual propagation to attest its genuineness." And he adds, what is of vast importance to bear in mind—" the Church must send her ablest, most highly educated, and best men to the heathen; . . . for the work in the foreign field is more difficult than the work at home;" and he describes as a " popular delusion " the supposition that " an army requires to be better led in peace than in war."

If these sketches help to attract attention,

* Dr. Livingstone.

to deepen sympathy, and to call forth help on behalf of this great cause,—more especially if they be the means of enlisting new warriors in this noblest of all services,—they will have answered the purpose for which they were written, and realized the prayer with which they are now sent forth.

W. P. O.

The Palace, Kilkenny.

December, 1881.

CONTENTS.

I.

As to the name that should stand foremost on the list of "Modern Heroes of the Mission-field," there can scarcely be a doubt. That of Henry Martyn does not, indeed, take the first place chronologically; for of those whose lives are to be sketched, one at least preceded him in the mission field; but for the saintliness of his character, the devotedness of his life, and the influence of his bright though brief career, his name stands confessedly pre-eminent.

It is most natural, and appropriate also, considering the purpose for which these sketches were written, that a member of the Church of England should enjoy this distinction ; and we have no doubt that Nonconformists themselves will rejoice to see

Martyn's name taking such a position on a roll which records the achievements of some of their own most distinguished missionaries. His claim to this place in our own ranks is unquestionable. What Herbert is amongst our poets, and Wilson amongst our bishops, Henry Martyn is amongst our missionary heroes. High Church, Low Church, Broad Church, or whatever other sections there may be amongst us, unite with one accord in giving their meed of honour to this most saintly of men. We cannot, indeed, go so far as Sir James Stephen, and say that "Martyn's is the one heroic name which adorns the annals of the English Church from the days of Elizabeth to our own;" but we can assign him a foremost place amongst our best and noblest worthies. Although, in respect to direct missionary success, his career must be considered as almost a failure, yet, in its indirect effects, no other has been more fruitful. His "Life" has awakened the missionary spirit in more human hearts than any other memoir ever given to the world; and not only has it stirred up many a brave spirit to follow him to the same great battle-field, but it has sustained and cheered many a soldier of the cross amidst his arduous conflicts. Thus Weitbrecht writes: "During my leisure hours I read Henry Martyn's life. Dear Martyn! how I love his tender heart and his intense love to his Saviour! If any reading besides the Bible is calculated to bring a missionary into a proper frame of mind, while engaged in his labour of love, it is the 'Life' of this holy man. It raised my mind to holy aspirations for the same spirit. Oh! how I can feel with him in griefs and sorrows, being tempted and tried by an unbelieving world much in the same way."

A valued friend whom I consulted in reference to these sketches said to me, "I fear the life of Henry Martyn is a hackneyed subject;" and in one sense he was right, for no story has been more frequently read, or is better known; but I do not think that the public are tired of it, and others are evidently of the same opinion; for there has lately issued from the press, as one of a series of books entitled " Men Worth Remembering," another sketch of our hero's life (by Canon Bell). This paper, however, does not pretend to be more than a loving " memorial " of one " whose praise is in all the churches," and a grateful record of labours which ought never to be forgotten.

Born (1781) in the humble home of one who had been a Cornish miner, but who, having learned the value of a little education for himself, desired to give a fuller measure of it to his son, Henry Martyn fought his way through difficulties and adversities up to the highest honours that his university could bestow. Cambridge may well be proud of her senior wrangler, and St. John's may well link together in honour the names of two illustrious students, who within her walls knew and loved each other; destined each of them to shine with an undying lustre, though in widely different spheres—Henry Kirke White as the poet, and Henry Martyn as the missionary.

How little we can determine, from his first attempts, concerning a man's future career may be illustrated from the fact that Martyn began his college studies by committing the propositions of Euclid to memory, and yet at the end of four short years he was the foremost mathematician of his class. It augured well for his many-sidedness of mind, that though he mainly applied himself to mathematics, he carried off the first prizes of his year in Latin composition, was elected fellow of his college, and was again and again appointed as Examiner in classics and metaphysics. Indeed, he was known amongst his fellow-students as "the man who had not lost an hour." But the time was at hand when he was to lay down all his honours at the Master's feet, and to consecrate all his abilities and attainments to that Master's service.

He had already realized the insufficiency of earthly honours to make him happy. He thus describes his own feelings at the moment when all men were applauding and many envying him: "I obtained my highest wishes, but was surprised to find that I grasped a shadow." It reminds us of

Edmund Burke's famous saying on the occasion of a great election: "What shadows we are, and what shadows we pursue!" But Martyn had begun the search after enduring happiness. The influence of his younger sister, combined with that of a college friend who had been formerly his school companion, had led him to the study of the Holy Scriptures; and the death of his father, which occurred just as his son had attained the highest summit of his ambition, deepened his religious impressions, and he soon found rest and satisfaction in the gospel of Jesus Christ. Up to this time he had resolved on going to "the law" as a profession, and had preferred it to entering the ministry, "chiefly," as he confesses, "because he would not consent to be poor for Christ's sake." But now a new ambition seized him, and he resolved not only to become a clergyman, but to devote his life to the work of God amongst the heathen. He accordingly offered himself, at the close of the year 1802, to the Church Missionary Society, and professed himself ready to go to any part of the world as a missionary of the cross of Christ.

This choice was mainly determined by two things; first, by an observation of the Rev. Charles Simeon, to whose ministry at Cambridge he had attached himself. This observation had reference to the wonderful benefits which had resulted from the labours of a *single* missionary (Dr. Carey) in India, and the young graduate could not divest his mind of the impression which it made. It haunted him day and night. Soon after this he was led to read an account of David Brainerd, who had devoted a short but noble life to the evangelization of the Red Indians; and this memoir not only confirmed his growing resolve to dedicate himself to missionary work, but often guided and cheered him afterwards, amidst his arduous labours in the East. Most truly may it be said that he became what Brainerd often wished to be,—"a flame of fire in the service of his God."

It must not be forgotten that at the time Henry Martyn came to this resolve the

position of a missionary was held in pity and
contempt—in pity by those who esteemed
their work as an earnest but wild enthusiasm
—in contempt by those who considered them
more in the light of fools than fanatics.   It
was the day when the authorities openly
opposed missionary effort in India, and when
a Governor-General declared that the man
who could be mad enough to speak of
religion to the natives would fire a pistol
into a magazine of gunpowder.   Our
missionary-designate had to encounter these
prejudices, and to learn that not even his
admitted talents or his academic distinctions
could save him from scorn and misconcep-
tion.   "Yet I desire," he writes, "to take
the ridicule of men with all meekness and
charity, looking forward to another world for
approbation and reward."   And this moreover was a life-long trial; for towards the
end of his career we find him repeating lines,
which were often upon his lips during his
seven years of incessant toil—

> " If on my face for Thy dear name
>   Shame and reproaches be,

> All hail reproach, and welcome shame,
>   If Thou remember me ! "

And yet, strange to say, it was not as a professed missionary that this most devoted of all missionaries found his way to the East. Just at this crisis of his history all his little patrimony was lost, and as his sister was involved in the disaster, it appeared scarcely justifiable to leave her unprovided for, so long as his presence in England could alleviate her distress. His friends, in order to meet the difficulty, procured him a chaplaincy in the East India Company's service, and it was avowedly in that capacity he went forth to foreign lands; but how he used his position to further the great aim of his life let his whole subsequent history declare; and in what spirit he received the appointment let the following extract from his journal testify :—" The prospect of this world's happiness gave me rather pain than pleasure, which convinced me that I had been running away from the world rather than overcoming it."   Let no one imagine, however, that it was without the deepest pangs to which an affectionate and sensitive nature can be subjected, that Henry Martyn found himself taking leave of honours and fame and friends at home, to encounter the unknown but certain trials of what he was determined should be a missionary career. He makes no secret of his feelings; and his letters and journals bear witness that he took his last look at England with an almost breaking heart: "I find by experience that I am as weak as water." They are touching words—all the more touching for their honesty and truthfulness.

And there was besides, in his case, "a beautiful sad story" of tender and deep attachment to one who seemed well worthy of him, but whose union to the man she loved was hindered both then and afterwards by circumstances upon which we have neither time nor heart to linger. It is very affecting, as one reads his memoir, to see how her image again and again rises to his view, now as he gazes from the deck of the vessel that bears him far away, or again as he looks out on the pale moonlight of an Eastern sky, or once more as he finds himself amidst the solitude and dreariness of some comfortless caravansary. The last letter he ever wrote was to Lydia Grenfell, when from his distant station at Tabriz, though labouring under illness and weakness, he looked forward to a meeting with her whom he hoped one day to call his wife. But it was not to be. Their union and their joy were to be reserved for heaven.

We cannot dwell upon the eventful voyage, during which, "instant in season and out of season," he preached Christ to his fellow-passengers, with a boldness that made some angry, and yet with a tenderness that made others weep. Nor can we stay to tell how on the Brazilian coast he gained alike the love of wealthy planter and of poor slave, and held conversations in Latin with priests and friars, endeavouring to win them to the "truth as it is in Jesus." Neither can we tarry to relate how at the Cape, where a fierce war was waging, he went ashore, regardless of all danger, to minister to the wounded and the dying, and to speak both to degraded Hottentot and brave British soldier the words of eternal life.

India was reached at last, and the heart of our missionary was filled with conflicting emotions—of joy, to find himself in the scene of his long-anticipated labours—of despondency, when he looked around and saw the " gross darkness " of the land, and the apparently insuperable hindrances in his path. With all his enthusiasm, he was not the man to under-estimate the difficulties of his work; and with a temperament which was not so much the result of melancholy as of an exquisite sensitiveness, his heart often sank within him at the scenes he witnessed, and the abominations by which he was surrounded. His righteous soul was vexed, now by the apathy or the opposition shown by his fellow-countrymen in India towards the truth which he preached; now by their ungodly lives, which raised up the most fearful stumbling-blocks against the reception of Christianity by the natives. At one time we find him saddened and depressed by gross idolatries in the pagoda of Juggernaut, at another horrified at finding himself just too late to rescue a deluded woman from the blazing fire of the Suttee. It was no marvel that he should say, "I shivered as if standing as it were in the neighbourhood of hell;" and again, "The fiends of darkness seem to sit in sullen repose in this land."

Still his faith failed not; he knew what God could do in His own good time, and in that confidence he wrote these almost prophetic words: "Even if I never should see a native converted, God may design, by my patience and continuance in the work, to encourage future missionaries."

His first home in India was appropriately enough in a ruined pagoda which was fitted up for his use, and it was a joy to him that "the place where once devils were worshipped was now become a Christian oratory." He soon made the acquaintance of men likeminded with himself—Brown and Corrie, and also of the Serampore missionaries—Carey and Marshman. He had really been given to India in answer to their prayers, and they were not slow to appreciate his character and worth. Indeed, every effort was made to detain him at Calcutta, that he might minister to the English, but his heart was set on his special work, and from the first he sedulously devoted himself to the acquisition of Sanscrit and Hindustani, in order to fit himself for it, often wearying his Munshees by his untiring assiduity.

At the end of four months he was sent to Dinapore, and began his regular duties as chaplain to the troops. To a man like Martyn these were not matters of mere routine; nor did he confine his ministrations to the ordinary services from the drum-head, or to the visitation of sick soldiers in the hospital. He had special meetings in the evening for such as were desirous of further spiritual instruction; he gathered the native wives of the soldiers every Sunday afternoon for a service in their own tongue; he prepared for their use a Hindustani translation of our Lord's parables, with a simple commentary; and he opened, at his own cost, five schools for native children. Frequently his duties were of a most painful kind. At one time he is remonstrating with a colonel who is living in open and flagrant sin; at another he is rebuking an apostate official who has abjured Christianity, and built a mosque in honour of the false prophet. But amidst all this his heart is fixed upon his chosen work; he is mastering Arabic and Persian; he is disputing with Brahmins, and becoming acquainted with their tenets; he is studying the Ramayuna and the Koran; he is translating portions of the New Testament and of the Prayer Book into oriental tongues; and all this in a place where, to use his own regretful language, "not one voice is heard saying, ' I wish you good luck · in the name of the Lord.'"

Three years of this prefatory work, and he is transferred to Cawnpore (1809), where we find him preaching to a thousand soldiers drawn up in a hollow square, when the heat is so intense that many of the men drop down around him, and where his own health suffers continually from ague and fever. It was here that he had the happiness of meet-ing Mrs. Sherwood, whose Christian sym

pathy cheered him, and whose graphic pen
has left us such vivid portraits both of our
hero and his work.   Her first impressions
of him are thus recorded : " He was dressed
in white, and looked very pale, which however was nothing singular in India; his hair,
a light brown, was raised from his forehead,
which was a remarkably fine one.   His
features were not regular, but the expression
was so luminous, so intellectual, so affectionate, so beaming with Divine charity, that no
one could have looked at his features and
thought of their shape or form; the out-
beaming of his soul would absorb the
attention of every observer."   She describes
him as most polished and refined; with a
voice and ear most musical; and her picture
of her little Lucy, eighteen months old,
creeping up to the pale, white-clad missionary, as he lay upon his sofa, with all his books
around him, and perching herself on the big
Hebrew Lexicon, which he needed at every
turn, but from which his gentle love would not
displace her, is most beautiful and touching,
and shows that his was not the morose and

gloomy temperament with which he has sometimes been unfairly credited.

It was at Cawnpore he made his first essay at public preaching to the natives; and his was a weird and motley congregation. On Sunday evenings he opened the gates of his garden to the devotees and vagrants who haunted the station, and who were easily induced to attend by the promise of a pice apiece. Sometimes from five to eight hundred of these Jogees and Fakeers would crowd around him, as he read to them some striking verse of Scripture, and then endeavoured to explain to them, in language most simple but most beautiful, the Fatherhood of God and the love of Jesus Christ our Saviour. It was a scene that might have inspired the pencil of some great artist. Mrs. Sherwood says that "no dreams in the delirium of a raging fever could surpass the realities" presented on these occasions. She describes this frightful crowd, "clothed with abominable rags, or nearly without clothes, or plastered with mud and cow-dung, or with long matted locks streaming down to their heels; every countenance foul and frightful with evil passions; the lips black with tobacco, or crimson with henna. One man who came in a cart, drawn by a bullock, was so bloated as to look like an enormous frog; another had kept an arm above his head, with his hand clenched till the nails had come out of the back of his hand; and one very tall man had all his bones marked on his dark skin with white chalk, like the figure of grim Death himself."

Such was the congregation of the gifted and accomplished Fellow of St. John's, but it realized to him the happy experience of the Master—"To the poor the gospel is preached;" and though at the time he only knew of one old Hindu woman (whom he had baptized) as the fruit of his labour, a seed had fallen in that unlikely place, which brought forth much fruit in after days. Amongst some young Mussulmans who sat one evening on the wall of the missionary's garden, amusing themselves with the "folly" of the English padre, was a pundit named Sheik Salah. To him the word of God proved quick and powerful, and we meet with him afterwards in mission history as Abdul Messeh, the earliest of our Indian pastors, who was ordained by Bishop Heber, and of whom that discerning and lamented prelate speaks in his journal with such commendation. More than forty Hindus were converted to Christianity by the instrumentality of this one man; and when he died, a monument was erected by the Resident at Lucknow, to commemorate his devotedness and success. Truly the labours of Henry Martyn were " not in vain in the Lord," although in this case, as in others, he was not privileged to see the fruits for himself.

But his great work was his translation of the New Testament, first into the Hindustani, and next into the Persian tongue. To use an expression of his own, he felt that " the translation of the Scriptures was the grand point," and that it would be " a work of more lasting benefit" than his preaching would be, and therefore to this he gave himself unremittingly. His assistant in the Hindustani translation was a famous scholar named Mirza, of Benares, who seems to have been a comfort as well as a help to him ; but Sabat, the Arabian, whom he employed to aid him in the Persian, and who afterwards became an apostate from Christianity, was a constant trouble and perplexity ; his wild, passionate nature breaking out perpetually into all kinds of insubordination. In one passage of his journal, Martyn speaks thus truly though unconsciously of his own spirit, when he says, " And this also I learnt, that the power of gentleness is irresistible." But not even Martyn's gentleness could tame this Ishmaelite ; and one result of his proud and unbending superciliousness was that the missionary's better judgment was often overborne in the work which he had in hand ; so that after the translation was completed he had the mortification of finding that whilst in the opinion of competent judges his Hindustani was all that could be desired, his Persian was too lofty in its style, and too full of Arabic idioms, to be generally useful. On making this discovery, he resolved to go into Persia and Arabia, with the view of revising his Persian Testament under the most favourable circumstances, and of completing an Arabic version which was nearly finished.

He quitted India in bad health. Symptoms of consumption, the hereditary disease of his family, had begun to show themselves, and his incessant toil had greatly enfeebled him. His friend, Mr. Browne (at whose instigation he first took up the work of translation), wrote to him, with oriental expressiveness, " Can I then bring myself to cut the string, and let you go? I confess I could not if your bodily frame were strong, and promised to last for half a century. But as you burn with the intenseness and rapid blaze of phosphorus, why should we not make the most of you? Your flame may last as long, and perhaps longer in Arabia, than in India. Where should the phœnix build her odoriferous nest, but in the land prophetically called the ' blessed ' ? And where should we ever expect but from that country the true Comforter to come to the nations of the East ? "

He left India on the 7th of January, 1811, without a companion, without even an attendant, and it is only from fragments of his letters and journals we can trace his progress. Now he is on board a vessel for Bombay, and delights in hearing from the captain, who had been a pupil of Schwartz, the story of that noble missionary; now he is standing by the tomb of Xavier at Goa, and visiting the chambers of the Inquisition close by; now he is suffering from sunstroke at Bushire; now he is traversing in oriental dress the mountain paths of Persia, with the thermometer rising to 126° at noon, and with the nights so piercingly cold that he has to gather all his wraps about him to keep himself from shivering—"a fire within my head, my skin like a cinder, my pulse violent." But as we read of the countless "parasangs" he travelled day after day, and contrast the object of his journey with that of a Cyrus or an Alexander, we cannot fail to see that the humble missionary was a truer hero than the mighty conquerors who preceded him in those classic regions. Arrived at Shiraz, "the Athens of Persia," he spent the last year of his brief eventful life in perfecting his New Testament, and translating the Book of Psalms. He sought to lay the precious volume, when completed, at the feet of the Shah, and travelled a thousand miles with this object; but fever struck him down before he could accomplish it, and the presentation had to be made by Sir Gore Ousley, the British ambassador. The gift was graciously accepted by the monarch; and better still, it was declared by the best judges to be "a noble version;" and having been printed afterwards at St. Petersburg, it went forth on the wings of the press in a tongue which, according to his biographer, "is spoken by 200,000 who bear the Christian name," and is known moreover to a large proportion of the earth's inhabitants.

Not, indeed, without manifold interruptions was this great work accomplished. Again and again had our missionary to encounter the Mollahs and the Soofies of Persia in public and private disputation. In these controversies all his faith and patience as a Christian, as well as all his acumen and learning as a scholar, were put to the severest test.   There is something grand as we look at that gentle and emaciated, but intrepid young man (he had scarcely passed his thirtieth year) encountering, single-handed, the fanaticism and the fury of these Eastern sages, and confessing and upholding the religion of Christ against the speculations of vain philosophy, and the blasphemies of Islam, when to do so was to run the risk of losing life.   To Henry Martyn, we believe, belongs the honour of having been the first in modern days to preach the gospel of Christ to the followers of the false prophet; and he did so with a tact and a skill which won the admiration of his opponents.   We must wait " until all things are made known " before we can tell the full issues of these discussions.   But Sir Robert Ker Porter has mentioned how earnestly he was asked, on his journey, by some Persians, whether he was acquainted with " the man of God." " He came here," they said, " in the midst of us, sat down encircled by our wise men, and made such remarks upon our Koran as cannot be answered. . . . We want to know more about his religion and the book that he left among us."

A writer in the *Asiatic Journal* has mentioned the case of an interesting and accomplished man, called Mahomed Rahem, whom he met at Shiraz, and who for years had been secretly a Christian. On inquiry, it turned out that he had been led to change his religious opinions in consequence, as he said, of the teaching of "a beardless youth enfeebled by disease," who had visited their city in the 1223 of the Hegira, and encountered their Mollahs with great ability and forbearance. He then described a farewell visit which he had paid to the young missionary before his departure from Shiraz, and said, " That visit sealed my conversion. He gave me a book; it has been my constant companion ; the study of it has formed my most delightful occupation ; its contents have consoled me." He showed the book. It was the New Testament in Persian, and on one of the blank leaves was written,

" There is joy in heaven over one sinner that repenteth.—HENRY MARTYN."

There is no mention of Mahomed Rahem in Martyn's memoir, but he was probably one of those young men who, as he says, came from the college, "full of zeal and logic," to try him with hard questions.

Soon after this his face was turned towards Europe. He resolved to make his way to England, *viâ* Constantinople, to recruit his failing health, and perhaps to bring back his beloved one with him to India. The fragments which record his last journey are painfully interesting. Shattered in health, enduring the severest privations, driven along with relentless haste in spite of failing strength by a heartless dragoman—" the merciless Hassan "—but bearing all with the spirit of a martyr and a saint, he lay down to die at Tocat, on the 16th of October, 1812, at the early age of thirty-one, without a friend to comfort him, without one Christian near to smooth his dying pillow, or to catch his parting words. Whether he died of exhaustion, or of the plague which was then raging, none can tell.

The last entry in his journal, ten days before his death, is this :—

" *Oct. 6th.*—No horses being to be had, I had an unexpected repose. I sat in the orchard, and thought with sweet comfort and peace of my God,—in solitude my Company, my Friend, and Comforter. Oh ! when shall time give place to eternity ? when shall appear that new heaven and that new earth wherein dwelleth righteousness ? There—there shall in nowise enter anything that defileth ; none of that wickedness which has made men worse than beasts ; none of those corruptions that add still more to the miseries of mortality shall be seen or heard of any more."

The love and piety of Christian brethren have in later years erected a suitable memorial over this true soldier of the cross. They found the rude slab that covered his grave concealed beneath the sand of a mountain stream, but so little was known of him, by those who had buried him, that it is said they had carved thereon the name of " *William Martyn.*" The remains were lovingly removed to a quiet spot in the mission cemetery, and help was obtained from the East India Company and other sources to build a handsome monument. The inscription in four different languages is as follows :—

REV. HENRY MARTYN, M.A.,

CHAPLAIN OF THE EAST INDIA COMPANY, BORN AT TRURO,
IN ENGLAND, ON THE 18TH FEBRUARY, 1781, DIED
AT TOCAT, ON THE 16TH OCTOBER, 1812.
HE LABOURED FOR MANY YEARS IN THE EAST, STRIVING
TO BENEFIT MANKIND, BOTH IN THIS WORLD
AND FOR THAT TO COME.
HE TRANSLATED THE HOLY SCRIPTURES INTO HINDUSTANI
AND PERSIAN, AND MADE IT HIS GREAT OBJECT
TO PROCLAIM TO ALL MEN THE GOD AND
SAVIOUR OF WHOM THEY TESTIFY.
HE WILL LONG BE REMEMBERED IN THE COUNTRIES
WHERE HE WAS KNOWN, AS "A MAN OF GOD."
MAY TRAVELLERS OF ALL NATIONS, AS THEY STEP ASIDE
AND LOOK ON THIS MONUMENT, BE LED TO HONOUR,
LOVE, AND SERVE THE GOD AND SAVIOUR OF
THIS DEVOTED MISSIONARY !

The gifted pen of Lord Macaulay has furnished another epitaph:—

" Here Martyn lies ! In manhood's early bloom
The Christian hero found a pagan tomb;
Religion, sorrowing o'er her favourite son,
Points to the glorious trophies which he won—
Eternal trophies, not with slaughter red,
Not stained with tears by hopeless captives shed,
But trophies of the Cross; for that dear name
Through every form of danger, death, and shame,
Onward he journeyed to a happier shore,
Where danger, death, and shame are known no more."

For ourselves, a prayer in one of his earliest journals seems best to express the wishes of our hearts, both with respect to the influence of his own memory, and of that higher example which ruled his life :—

"Memoria tua sancta, et dulcedo tua beatissima possideant animam meam, atque in invisibilium amorem rapiant illam."

II.

THERE is a story told about the subject of the following sketch which may be repeated here by way of introduction. It is said that long after he had attained to fame and eminence in India, being Professor of oriental languages in the college of Fort William, honoured with letters and medals from royal hands, and able to write F.L S., F.G.S., F.A.S., and other symbols of distinction after his name, he was dining one day with a select company at the Governor-General's, when one of the guests, with more than questionable taste, asked an aide-de-camp present, in a whisper loud enough to be heard by the professor, whether Dr. Carey had not once been a shoemaker. "No, sir," immediately answered the doctor, "only a cobbler!" Whether he was proud of it, we cannot say; that he had no need to be ashamed of it, we are sure. He had outlived the day when Edinburgh reviewers tried to heap contempt on "consecrated cobblers," and he had established his right to be enrolled amongst the aristocracy of learning and philanthropy.

Some fifty years before this incident took place, a visitor might have seen over a small shop in a Northamptonshire village a signboard with the following inscription:—

SECOND-HAND SHOES BOUGHT AND SOLD.

WILLIAM CAREY.

The owner of this humble shop was the son of a poor schoolmaster, who inherited a taste for learning; and though he was consigned to the drudgery of mending boots and shoes, and was even then a sickly, careworn man, in poverty and distress, with a delicate and unsympathizing wife, he lost no opportunity of acquiring information both in languages and natural history, and taught himself drawing and painting. He always worked with lexicons and classics open upon his bench; so that Scott, the commentator, to whom it is said that he owed his earliest religious impressions, used to call that shop "Mr. Carey's college." His tastes—we ought rather to say God's providence—soon led him to open a village school; and as he belonged to the Baptist community, he combined with the office of schoolmaster that of a preacher in their little chapel at Moulton, with the scanty salary of £16 a year. Strange to say, it was whilst giving his daily lessons in geography that the flame of missionary zeal was kindled in his bosom. As he looked upon the vast regions depicted on the map of the world, he began to ponder on the spiritual darkness that brooded over so many of them, and this led him to collect and collate information on the subject, until his whole mind was occupied with the absorbing theme.

It so happened that a gathering of Baptist ministers at Northampton invited a subject for discussion, and Carey, who was present, at once proposed "The duty of Christians to attempt the spread of the Gospel amongst heathen nations." The proposal fell amongst them like a bombshell, and the young man was almost shouted down by those who thought such a scheme impracticable and wild. Even Andrew Fuller, who eventually became his great supporter, confessed that he found himself ready to exclaim, "If the Lord would make windows in heaven, might this thing be?" But Carey's zeal was not to be quenched. He brought forward the topic again and again; he wrote a pamphlet on the subject; and on his removal to a more important post of duty at Leicester, he won over several influential persons to his views. It was at this time (1792) he preached his famous sermon from Isaiah liv. 2, 3, and summed up its teaching in these two important statements : (1) "Expect great things from God," and (2) "Attempt great things for God." This led to the formation of the Baptist Missionary Society; and Carey, at the age of thirty-three, proved his sincerity by volunteering to be its first messenger to the heathen. Andrew Fuller had said, " There is a gold mine in India ; but it seems as deep as the centre of the earth ; who will venture to explore it ? " " I will go down," responded William Carey, in words never to be forgotten, " but remember that you must hold the rope." The funds of the Society amounted at the time to £13 2s. 6d.

But the chief difficulties did not arise out of questions of finance. The East India Company, sharing the jealousy against missionary effort, which, alas ! at that time was to be found amongst the chief states-men of the realm, and amongst prelates of the Established Church as well as amongst Nonconformist ministers, were opposed to all such efforts, and no one could set his foot upon the Company's territory without a special licence. The missionary party and their baggage were on board the *Earl of Oxford*, and the ship was just ready to sail, when an information was laid against the captain for taking a person on board without an order from the Company, and forthwith the passengers and their goods were hastily put on shore, and the vessel weighed anchor for Calcutta, leaving them behind, disappointed and disheartened.

They returned to London. Mr. Thomas, who was Carey's companion and brother missionary, went to a coffee-house, when, to use his own language, "to the great joy of a bruised heart, the waiter put a card into my hand, whereon were written these life-giving words: '*A Danish East Indiaman, No.* 10, *Cannon Street.*' No more tears that night. Our courage revived; we fled to No. 10, Cannon Street, and found it was the office of Smith and Co., agents, and that Mr. Smith was a brother of the captain's; that this ship had sailed, as he supposed, from Copenhagen; was hourly expected in Dover roads; would make no stay there; and the terms were £100 for each passenger, £50 for a child, and £25 for an attendant." This of course brought up the financial difficulty in a new and aggravated form; but the generosity of the agent and owner of the ship soon overcame it, and within twenty-four hours of their return to London, Mr. Carey and his party embarked for Dover; and on the 13th June, 1793, they found themselves on board the *Kron Princessa Maria*, where they were treated with the utmost kindness by the captain, who admitted them to his own table, and provided them with special cabins.

The delay, singularly enough, removed one of Carey's chief difficulties and regrets. His wife, who was physically feeble, and whose deficiency, in respect to moral intrepidity, was afterwards painfully accounted for by twelve years of insanity in India, had positively refused to accompany him, and he had consequently made up his mind to go out alone. She was not with him when he and his party were suddenly expelled from the English ship; but she was so wrought upon by all that had occurred, as well as by renewed entreaties, that with her sister and her five children she set sail with him for Calcutta.

Difficulties of various kinds surrounded them upon their arrival in India. Poverty, fevers, bereavement, the sad illness of his wife, the jealousy of the Government, all combined to render it necessary that for a while Carey should betake himself to an employment in the Sunderbunds, where he had often to use his gun to supply the wants of his family; and eventually he went to an indigo factory at Mudnabully, where he hoped to earn a livelihood. But he kept the grand project of his life distinctly in view; he set himself to the acquisition of the language, he erected schools, he made missionary tours, he began to translate the New Testament, and above all he worked at his printing press, which was set up in one corner of the factory, and was looked upon by the natives as his god.

Carey's feelings at this time with regard to his work will be best expressed in the following passage from a letter to his sisters: "I know not what to say about the mission. I feel as a farmer does about his crop; sometimes I think the seed is springing, and then I hope; a little time blasts all, and my hopes are gone like a cloud. . . . I preach every day to the natives, and twice on the Lord's Day constantly, besides other itinerant labours; and I try to speak of Jesus Christ and Him crucified, and of Him alone; but my soul is often dejected to see no fruit." And then he goes on to speak of that department of his labour in which his greatest achievements were ultimately to be won: " The work of translation is going on, and I hope the whole New Testament and the five books of Moses may be completed before this reaches you. It is a pleasant work and a rich reward, and I trust, whenever it is published, it will soon prevail, and put down all the Shastras of the Hindus. . . . The translation of the Scriptures I look upon to be one of the greatest desiderata in the world, and it has accordingly occupied a considerable part of my time and attention."

Five or six years of patient unrequited toil passed by, and then four additional labourers were sent out by the Society to Carey's help. Two of them will never be forgotten, and the names of Carey, Marsh-

man, and Ward will ever be inseparably
linked in the history of Indian missions.
Ward had been a printer; and it was a
saying of Carey's, addressed to him in
England, that led him to adopt a missionary's life: "We shall want you," said he,
"in a few years, to print the Bible; you
must come after us." Marshman had been
an assistant in a London book-shop, but
soon found that his business there was not
to his taste, as he wished to know more
about the contents of books than about their
covers; so he set up a school at Bristol,
mastered Greek and Latin, Hebrew and
Syriac, and became prosperous in the world;
but he gave up all to join Carey in his
noble enterprise, and moreover, brought out
with him, as a helper in the mission, a young
man whom he himself had been the means
of converting from infidelity. Marshman's
wife was a cultivated woman, and her
boarding school in India brought in a
good revenue to the mission treasury. His
daughter married Henry Havelock, who
made for himself as great a name in the

military annals of his country as his illustrious father-in-law had won for himself in the missionary history of the world.

The jealous and unchristian policy of the East India Company would not allow the newly arrived missionaries to join their brethren, and they were compelled to seek shelter under a foreign flag. Fortunately for the cause of missions, a settlement had been secured by the Danes at Serampore, some sixteen miles up the river from Calcutta, and it now proved "a city of refuge" to Englishmen who had been driven from territory which owned the British sway. The governor of the colony, Colonel Bie, was a grand specimen of his race; he had been in early days a pupil of Schwartz, and he rejoiced in knowing that the kings of Denmark had been the first Protestant princes that ever encouraged missions amongst the heathen. He gave the exiled missionaries a generous welcome, and again and again gallantly resisted all attempts to deprive them of his protection, declaring that "if the British Government still refused

to sanction their continuance in India, they
should have the shield of Denmark thrown
over them if they would remain at Serampore." Carey determined, though it was
accompanied with personal loss to himself,
to join his brethren at Serampore, and the
mission soon was organized in that place,
which became, so to speak, " the cradle of
Indian missions." It possessed many advantages: it was only sixty miles from
Nuddea, and was within a hundred of the
Mahratta country; here the missionaries
could preach the Gospel and work their
printing press without fear, and from this
place they could pass under Danish pass-
ports to any part of India. There was a
special providence in their coming to Serampore at the time they did; for in 1801 it
passed over to English rule without the
firing of a shot.

They were soon at work, both in their
schools and on their preaching tours.
Living on homely fare, and working for
their bread, they went forth betimes in pairs
to preach the word of the living God, now

in the streets or in the bazaars, now in the midst of heathen temples, attracting crowds to hear them by the sweet hymns which Carey had composed in the native tongue, and inviting inquirers to the mission-house for further instruction. The first convert was baptized in the same year, on the day after Christmas. His name was Krishnu. He had been brought to the mission-house for medical relief, and was so influenced by what he saw and heard, that he resolved to become a Christian. On breaking caste by eating with the missionaries, he was seized by an enraged mob, and dragged before the magistrate, but to their dismay he was released from their hands. Carey had the pleasure of performing the ceremony of baptism with his own hands, in presence of the governor and a crowd of natives and Europeans. It was his first recompence after seven years of toil, and it soon led the way to other conversions. Amongst the rest, a high-caste Brahmin divested himself of his sacred thread, joined the Christian ranks, and preached the faith which he once destroyed. Krishnu became an efficient helper, and built at his own expense the first place of worship for native Christians in Bengal. Writing about him twelve years after his baptism, Carey says, "He is now a steady, zealous, well-informed, and I may add eloquent minister of the Gospel, and preaches on an average twelve or fourteen times every week in Calcutta and its neighbourhood."

But we must turn from the other labourers and the general work of the mission to dwell upon the special work for which Carey's tastes and qualifications so admirably fitted him. We have seen that his heart was set on the translation and printing of the Scriptures, and to this from the outset he sedulously devoted himself. On the 17th March, 1800, the first sheet of the Bengali New Testament was ready for the press, and in the next year Carey was able to say, "I have lived to see the Bible translated into Bengali, and the whole New Testament printed." But this was far from being the end of Carey's enterprise. In 1806, the

Serampore missionaries contemplated and issued proposals for rendering the Holy Scriptures into fifteen oriental languages, viz., Sanscrit, Bengali, Hindustani, Persian, Mahratta, Guzarathi, Oriya, Kurnata, Te-linga, Burman, Assam, Boutan, Thibetan, Malay, and Chinese. Professor Wilson, the Boden Professor of Sanscrit at Oxford, has told us how this proposal was more than accomplished: "They published," he says, "in the course of about five-and-twenty years, translations of portions of the Old and New Testament, more or less consider-able, in forty different dialects." It is not pretended that they were conversant with all these forms of speech, but they employed competent natives, and as they themselves were masters of Sanscrit and several ver-nacular dialects, they were able to guide and superintend them.

In all this work Dr. Carey (for the degree of Doctor of Divinity had been bestowed on him by a learned university) took a leading part. Possessed of at least six different dialects, a thorough master of the Sanscrit, which is the parent of the whole family, and gifted besides with a rare genius for philological investigation, "he carried the project," says the professor, "to as successful an issue as could have been expected from the bounded faculties of man." And when it is remembered that he began his work at a time when there were no helps or appliances for his studies; when grammars and dictionaries of these dialects were unknown, and had to be constructed by himself; when even manuscripts of them were scarce, and printing was utterly unknown to the natives of Bengal, the work which he not only set before him, but accomplished, must be admitted to have been Herculean. Frequently did he weary out three pundits in the day, and to the last hour of his life he never intermitted his labours. The following apology for not engaging more extensively in correspondence will be read with interest, and allowed to be a sufficient one :—" I translate from Bengali and from Sanscrit into English. Every proof-sheet of the Bengali and Mahratta Scriptures must go three times at least through my hands. A dictionary of the Sanscrit goes once at least through my hands. I have written and printed a second edition of the Bengali grammar, and collected materials for a Mahratta dictionary. Besides this, I preach twice a week, frequently thrice, and attend upon my collegiate duties. I do not mention this because I think my work a burden—it is a real pleasure—but to show that my not writing many letters is not because I neglect my brethren, or wish them to cease writing to me."

Carey was by no means a man of brilliant genius, still less was he a man of warm enthusiasm; he had nothing of the sentimental, or speculative, or imaginative in his disposition; but he was a man of untiring energy and indomitable perseverance. Difficulties seemed only to develop the one and to increase the other. These difficulties arose from various quarters, sometimes from the opposition of the heathen, sometimes from the antagonism of the British

Government, sometimes, and more painfully, from the misapprehensions or injudiciousness of the Society at home; but he never was dismayed. On the contrary, he gathered arguments for progress from the opposition that was made to it. "There is," he writes "a very considerable difference in the appearance of the mission, which to me is encouraging. The Brahmins are now most inveterate in their opposition; they oppose the Gospel with the utmost virulence, and the very name of Jesus Christ seems abominable in their ears." And all this is the more remarkable, when we remember that he was by nature indolent. He says of himself, "No man ever living felt inertia to so great a degree as I do." He was in all respects a man of principle, and not of impulse. Kind and gentle, he was yet firm and unwavering. Disliking compliments and commendations for himself, it was not his habit to bestow them upon others. Indeed, he tells us that the only attempt which he ever made to pay a compliment met with such discouragement, that he never had any inclination to renew the attempt. A nephew of the celebrated President Edwards called upon him with a letter of introduction, and Carey congratulated him on his relationship to so great a personage; but the young man dryly replied, "True, sir, but every tub must stand on its own bottom."

From his childhood he had been in earnest in respect to anything he undertook. He once tried to climb a tree and reach a nest, but failed, and soon came to the ground; yet, though he had to limp home bruised and wounded, the first thing he did, when able again to leave the house, was to climb that same tree and take that identical nest. This habit of perseverance followed him through life. One evening, just before the missionaries retired to rest, the printing office was discovered to be on fire, and in a short time it was totally destroyed. Buildings, types, paper, proofs, and, worse than all, the Sanscrit and other translations perished in the flames. Ten thousand pounds' worth of property was destroyed that night, no portion of which was covered by insurance; but under the master mind of Carey the disaster was soon retrieved. A portion of the metal was recovered from the wreck, and as the punches and matrices had been saved, the types were speedily recast. Within two months the printers were again at their work; within two more the sum required to repair the premises had been collected; and within seven the Scriptures had been re-translated into the Sanscrit language. Carey preached on the next Lord's-day after the conflagration, from the text, " Be still, and know that I am God," and set before his hearers two thoughts: (1) God has a sovereign right to dispose of us as He pleases; (2) we ought to acquiesce in all that God does with us and to us. Writing to a friend at this time, he calmly remarks that " travelling a road the second time, however painful it may be, is usually done with greater ease and certainty than when we travel it for the first time." To such a man success was already assured, and by such a man success was well deserved. And it came.

When the Government looked round for a suitable man to fill the chair of oriental languages in their college at Fort William, their choice fell, almost as a necessity, upon the greatest scholar in India, and so the persecuted missionary became the honoured Professor of Sanscrit, Bengali, and Mahratta, at one thousand rupees a month. He stipulated, however, that he would accept the office only on the condition that his position as a missionary should be recognized ; and he took a noble revenge upon those who had so long opposed his work, by devoting the whole of his newly-acquired salary to its further extension. His new position served to call attention to missionary work ; and by degrees a better feeling sprang up towards it both at home and abroad. Carey and his companions were at length able to preach in the bazaars of Calcutta. Fresh labourers had come to India. Corrie, Browne, Martyn, and Buchanan were stirring the depths of Christian sympathy by their work and by their appeals. Grant, Wilberforce, and Macaulay were rousing the British nation to some faint sense of duty; so that when the charter of the East India Company came to be renewed in 1813, the restrictive regulations were defeated in the House of Commons by a majority of more than two to one. In the very next year the foundations of the Indian Episcopate were laid; and in the following year Dr. Middleton, the first Metropolitan of India (having Ceylon for one archdeaconry, and Australia for another!) was visiting the Serampore missionaries, in company with the Governor-General, and expressing his admiration and astonishment at their work.

Distinctions crowded fast upon the Northamptonshire cobbler. Learned societies thought themselves honoured by admitting him to membership. He had proved himself a useful citizen, as well as a devoted missionary. He had established a botanic garden, and edited " The Flora Indica; " he had founded an agricultural society, and was elected its president; he suggested a plantation committee for India, and was its most active member; he collected a splendid museum of natural history, which he bequeathed to his college; he was an early associate of the Asiatic Society, and contributed largely to its researches; he had translated the "Ramayana," the most ancient poem in the Sanscrit language, into three volumes; he was a constant writer in the *Friend of India;* he founded a college of his own, and obtained for it a royal charter from the King of Denmark; and in these and other ways he helped forward the moral and political reforms which have done so much for Hindustan. He was one of the first to memorialize the Government against the horrid infanticides at Sangor, and he lived to see them put down. He was early in the field to denounce the murderous abominations of the Suttee, and to oppose to them the authority even of the Hindu Vedas, and he had the satisfaction of seeing them abolished by Lord William Bentinck. He protested all along against the pilgrim tax, and the support afforded by

the Bengal Government to the worship of
Juggernaut, and he did not die until he
saw the subject taken up by others who
carried it to a triumphant issue.   What
would have been his devout gratitude, had
he lived to see the last links of connection
between the Government and the idol
temples severed in 1840, and Hindu and
Mohammedan laws, which inflicted for-
feiture of all civil rights on those who
became Christians, abrogated by the Lex
Loci Act of 1850!   What would have been
the joy of Carey, of Martyn, or of Corrie,
could they have heard the testimony borne
to the character and success of missions in
India by Sir Richard Temple, the late
Governor of Madras, at a public meeting
held last year in Birmingham!   He said,
"I have governed a hundred and five
millions of the inhabitants of India, and I
have been concerned with eighty-five millions
more in my official capacity. . . . I have
thus had acquaintance with, or been authen-
tically informed regarding, nearly all the
missionaries of all the societies labouring

in India within the last forty years. . . .
And what is my testimony concerning these
men? They are most efficient as pastors
of their native flocks, and as evangelists in
preaching in cities and villages from one
end of India to the other. In the work of
converting the heathen to the knowledge
and practice of the Christian religion, they
show great learning in all that relates to the
native religion and to the caste system. . . .
They are, too, the active and energetic
friends of the natives in all times of danger
and emergency."

So far as to the character of the missionaries. Speaking of their success, he said,
" It has sometimes been stated in the public
prints, which speak with authority, that their
progress has been arrested. Now, is this
really the case? Remember that missionary
work in India began in the year 1813, or
sixty-seven years ago. There are in the
present year not less than 350,000 native
Christians, besides 150,000 scholars, who,
though not all Christians, are receiving
Christian instruction; that is, 500,000 people,

or half a million, brought under the influence of Christianity. And the annual rate of increase in the number of native Christians has progressed with advancing years. At first it was reckoned by hundreds yearly, then by thousands, and further on by tens of thousands. . . . But it will be asked, what is the character of these Christian converts in India? what practically is their conduct as Christians? Now, I am not about to claim for them any extreme degree of Christian perfection. But speaking of them as a class, I venture to affirm that the Christian religion has exercised a dominant influence over their lives, and has made a decided mark on their conduct. They adhere to their faith under social difficulties. Large sacrifices have to be made by them. . . . The number of apostates may almost be counted on the fingers. . . . There is no such thing as decay in religion, nor any retrogression towards heathenism. On the contrary, they exhibit a laudable desire for the self-support and government of their Church. . . . I believe that if hereafter, during any revolution, any attempts were to be made by secular violence to drive the native Christians back from their religion, many of them would attest their faith by martyrdom."

Carey was not the man to wish or to expect that Government should step out of its sphere in order to enforce Christianity upon the natives. "Do you not think, Dr. Carey," asked a Governor-General, "that it would be wrong to force the Hindus to be Christians?" "My Lord," was the reply, "the thing is impossible; we may, indeed, force men to be hypocrites, but no power on earth can force men to become Christians." Carey, however, was too clear-headed not to see, and too honest not to say, that it was one thing to profess neutrality, and another to sanction idolatry; that it was one thing to abstain from using earthly power to propagate truth, and quite another to thwart rational and scriptural methods of diffusing it. And he was too much of a statesman, as well as too much of a missionary, not to see that in respect to some tenets of the Hindu system it would be impossible for the Government eventually to remain neutral, inasmuch as they subverted the very foundations upon which all government is based.

Such was the man who in the sequel won deserved honour even from hostile critics, and earned high encomiums from even prejudiced judges. Well might Lord Wellesley, who was, perhaps, the greatest of Indian statesmen, say concerning him, after listening to the first Sanscrit speech ever delivered in India by an European, and hearing that in it Carey had recognized his noble efforts for the good of India, "I esteem such a testimony from such a man a greater honour than the applause of courts and parliaments."

Still, amidst all his labours and all his honours, he kept the missionary enterprise distinctly in view, and during the forty years of his residence in India he gave it the foremost place. Several opportunities and no small inducements for returning to his native land were presented to him, but he declined them all. " I account this my own country," he said, "and have not the least inclination to leave it;" and he never did. To the last his translations of the Scriptures and his printing press were his chief care and his chief delight. He counted it so sacred a work, that he believed that a portion of the Lord's-day could not be better employed than in correcting his proof-sheets. In his seventy-third year, when weak from illness and old age, and drawing near to death, he writes, " I am now only able to sit and to lie upon my couch, and now and then to read a proof-sheet of the Scriptures; but I am too weak to walk more than across the house, nor can I stand even a few minutes without support." His last work was to revise his Bengali Bible, and on completing it he says, " There is scarcely anything for which I desired to live a little longer so much as for that."

He went back to Serampore to die; and " he died in the presence of all his brethren." It must have been a touching sight to see Dr. Wilson, the Metropolitan of India, standing by the death-bed of the dying Baptist, and asking for his blessing. It bore witness to the large-heartedness both of the prelate and of the missionary, and was a scene that did honour alike to the living and to the dying. Carey in his will directed that his funeral should be as plain as possible; that he should be laid in the same grave with his second wife, the accomplished Charlotte Rumohr, who had been a real helper to him in his work; and that on the simple stone which marked his grave there should be placed this inscription, and no more:—

WILLIAM CAREY,

Born August 17th, 1761 ; died ————.

Loving hands filled up the blank with "*the 9th June*, 1834." Before he died he had the privilege of seeing three of his sons engaged in the work to which he had devoted his own life. The name of one of them will meet us in another field of labour. He had aided in the establishment of more than thirty different missionary stations in various parts of India, and these were ministered to by some fifty pastors, one half of whom were natives of the country. He had seen a goodly number of converts gathered from heathenism into the Christian fold; and he had provided for them, and for multitudes who were to follow, the sacred Scriptures in their own divers tongues.

He sleeps in the mission burial ground of Serampore, beside Ward and Marshman. Ward had preceded him to the blessed rest by some eleven years, Marshman survived him by only three. They had lived and worked together in the midst of trial and opposition, for a quarter of a century, and they had learned to love one another as brothers. They had " coveted no man's silver or gold or apparel; " their " own hands had ministered to their necessities." " Marshman," says his biographer, " died like his colleagues, in graceful poverty, having devoted little short of £40,000 to the mission, through a long life of privation. " Their motives and their support amidst all their difficulties and dangers may be summed up in the following lines, which were written by Ward on his arrival at Serampore :—

"Lord, we are safe beneath Thy shade,
  And so shall be 'midst India's heat;
What should a missionary dread,
  Since devils crouch at Jesus' feet?

"There, blessed Saviour, let Thy cross
  Win many Hindu hearts to Thee;
This shall make up for every loss,
  Whilst Thou art ours eternally."

Speaking of this illustrious triumvirate, a dignitary of our Church in India has said, "There were only a few men at Serampore, but they were all giants." Other and distinguished missionaries succeeded them in their labours, but it is no disparagement to apply to them the language used concerning David's mighty men: "Howbeit they attained not unto the first three;" and we may add concerning Carey, what is said of the Tachmonite, "He sat in the seat, the chief amongst the captains."

III.

AMERICA has taken a prominent place in modern missionary effort. For a century and a half she had been engaged in desultory efforts for the heathen on her own continent, and men like Elliott and Brainerd had done a noble work for the perishing Red Indians. But the beginning of this century witnessed a grand outburst of missionary spirit beyond the Atlantic, and this spirit soon carried its messengers east and west across the waters to the shores of the Old World, where now they are to be found rivalling both in numbers and in zeal their elder European brethren.   Burmah, India, China, Africa, and the Isles of the Pacific bear witness to their labours; the Turkish Empire stands pre-eminently indebted to their efforts; and Lord Stratford de Redcliffe has borne such a testimony to what he saw and knew of American missionaries in Syria, Armenia, and Kurdistan, as proves their title to a distinguished place amongst the warriors of the cross.

Adoniram Judson (born in 1788, in the home of a Congregationalist minister in Massachusetts), as he was amongst the first of his countrymen to feel this new impulse, so was he confessedly the foremost in imparting it to others. The mission to Burmah, which was the first outcome of this awakened zeal, and in some respects the greatest and noblest field of its victories, must always be identified with him, and with those three illustrious women who were successively his wives, and whose names and labours must for ever be inseparably linked with his. In reading the eventful story of the Judsons, so full of peril and of patience, so marked by suffering and success, we seem as if we had alighted upon some grand romance; but we rise from its perusal with a deep conviction of its stern reality, and with a growing admiration of the Christian heroism which it displays.

Judson, as it has been well said, was "a missionary of the apostolic school." Like others who have led the van in the assaults of the Gospel upon paganism, he was a man pre-eminently endowed both by nature and by grace for the great work in which Providence employed him. We shall find, as a rule, that it is not the intellectually halt and feeble who have been called to "jeopard their lives unto the death in the high places of the field," and that the men who have gained this high distinction have moreover been baptized in a remarkable degree "with the Holy Ghost and with power." Such was Judson. The early precocity of his genius may be gathered from the fact that at three years of age he could read; that before he was ten he had gained a reputation for solving difficult arithmetical problems; and that when he entered college at sixteen, he obtained the highest place. Bright, intellectual, and enthusiastic, he was moreover extravagantly ambitious. His father had said one day that "he would be a great man," and a great man he resolved to be.

He dreamt of being a statesman, an orator, a poet, and he built his castles in the air accordingly; but he was far nearer the truth when, at four years of age, he used to collect the village children around him, and, mounted upon a chair, would preach to them a simple gospel with singular earnestness. His father and mother remembered in after years that the favourite hymn with which he prefaced these infant exercises was one beginning with the prophetic words—

"Go preach my Gospel, saith the Lord."

Brought up in a pious home, he had been visited by serious thoughts; but religion seemed to stand in the way of his ambition, and the wave of French infidelity reached him through the influence of a brilliant but sceptical fellow-student. Judson's thoughts and plans became consequently unsettled. Now we find him teaching a school at Plymouth, now attaching himself to a dramatic company, now touring in search of excitement through the Northern States. It was during this tour that God rescued him from infidelity and sin. He had reached a country inn, and the landlord apologized for putting him to sleep in the next room to that of a young man who was dying, but he had none other to offer him. Sad sounds came from that sick chamber through the midnight hours, and they stirred up solemn thoughts and anxious inquiries in Judson's breast. He made the case of that young man his own, and as he did so he felt the shallowness of his own newly-adopted philosophy, and its insufficiency to sustain him in the hour of death. The morning dawned, and he inquired about the sufferer. "He is dead." He asked his name, and was stunned at finding that it was that of his friend—shall we not rather say of his tempter? That morning he turned his horse's head towards home; God had begun a work in his heart, which resulted in true conversion. Soon we find him in the calm retirement of the Theological School at Andover, patiently inquiring into the truth of God, and ultimately yielding himself to Christ with a fulness of conviction and satisfaction, which never afterwards during his life was harassed by a single doubt.

Two years had scarcely passed by since that memorable night at the wayside inn. His father was now a pastor at Plymouth, and had conceived plans for his son's preferment.   The minister of the largest church at Boston was willing to take young Judson as a colleague, and the parents, delighted at the prospect, complacently apprised him of the good news.   "You will be so near home," said the mother.   But Judson did not speak.   His sister chimed in with her congratulations; and then the young man found a tongue, and earnestly replied, "No, sister, I shall never live in Boston; I have much farther to go."   Two years before he had startled them by the announcement of his infidel opinions; they were scarcely less startled now, though in a strangely different way, by hearing his firm resolve to be a missionary to the heathen.

How had it come about?   He had met with Buchanan's "Star in the East," and this had awakened the missionary spirit.

He had read Syme's "Embassy to Ava," and this had turned his whole soul towards Burmah and its benighted Buddhists. The leaven of missionary enterprise had begun to work in the Andover seminary. Three young men—their names deserve to be recorded—Mills, Richards, and Rice—had formed themselves into a missionary society in the college, with the object of training themselves for work amongst the heathen. Judson joined them, and soon became the leading spirit of the devoted band. Some one asked him in later life, during a visit to America, whether he had been more influenced by *faith* or *love* in going to Burmah. He paused a moment, and then replied, "There was in me at that time *little of either;* but in thinking of what *did* influence me, I remember a time out in the woods behind Andover seminary, when I was almost disheartened. Everything looked dark. No one had gone out from this country. The way was not open. The field was far distant, and in an unhealthy climate. I knew not what to do. All at once Christ's 'last command' seemed to come to my heart directly from heaven. I could doubt no longer, but, determined on the spot to obey it at all hazards, for the sake of *pleasing the Lord Jesus Christ.*" And then he added these memorable words, "If the Lord wants you for missionaries, He will send that word home to your hearts. If He does so, *you neglect it at your peril!*"

Out of that little group of students, as from a fruitful germ, grew up "The American Board of Commissioners for Foreign Missions," and Judson was their earliest and noblest agent. But first he was sent to England (in 1811) to confer with the London Missionary Society, and on the way was captured by a French privateer, and confined with other prisoners in the hold. Here, as he was translating from his Hebrew Bible into Latin, the doctor discovered him, and contrived his release from this part of the vessel. Landed at Bayonne, he was marched as a prisoner through the streets, and attracted the attention of a fellow-countryman by exclaiming against the injustice of detaining an American. This kindly citizen visited the dungeon to which Judson had been consigned, and managed to pass the prisoner out under the capacious folds of his own great cloak. Eventually Judson made his way to England, where he was kindly received, and whence he was promised help; but this foreign aid was not needed, for the American Board of Missions had already attracted large support, and Judson soon re-crossed the Atlantic, and was set apart for his grand enterprise. He was to go to some Asiatic field—in India or Burmah, according as God's providence should point the way. On the 5th February, 1812, he married the beautiful Anne Hasseltine; twelve days later he embarked with her for Calcutta, and on the 17th of June they reached their destination.

And here began the link with Serampore and the strange events which led to the formation of the Burmese mission. Carey and his fellow-labourers invited them to stay at the mission-house; and as Judson's views on baptism had undergone a change during the voyage out, he severed his connection with the American Board, and resolved to cast in his lot with the Baptist missionaries. But the East India Company, hostile to their work, and alarmed at this new influx of missionary labourers, issued a peremptory order that they should return to their own country. It so happened that a Mr. Chater. and Felix Carey (a son of the famous Serampore missionary) had gone a short time previously to Rangoon, to pioneer a way for missions in the empire of "the Golden Sovereign of land and water." It was decided to send the new-comers thither ; but even this could be effected only by stratagem. They were smuggled on board a vessel for the Mauritius, but were detected, and forced to disembark ; they contrived to get on board again, and on reaching St. Louis found that they must visit Madras as the only way of reaching Burmah. Here they narrowly escaped from another order of the Company, and eventually in a crazy vessel reached Rangoon in July 1813, half dead with sickness and discomfort.

It was a disheartening and a gloomy prospect that lay before them. There was at this time no provision made for their support. They were in a land of slaves ruled over by a despotic tyrant, and by rapacious viceroys, who were well called "the eaters of the provinces." Brutal murders and audacious robberies were of continual occurrence. The mission-house was close to the spot where public executions were constantly taking place. All around rose the gilded pagodas where the great Gaudama, as an incarnation of Buddha, was adored. In every street were seen the lamasaries, or homes of the priests, who were reckoned to be one in every thirty of the population, and who taught the cheerless creed of "Nirwana," or annihilation. Very few had so much as heard the name of Jesus, and it was death, according to the law, to renounce the faith of Buddha, which, alas! is still the dreary creed of three hundred millions of the earth's inhabitants. No marvel then that Judson and his wife should record that their first day in Burmah was "the most gloomy and distressing " that ever they had passed.

But the devoted pair set to work at once, applying themselves to the acquisition of the spoken tongue and of Pali, which is, so to speak, the sacred text of Ava. Like all true Protestant missionaries, Judson felt that if he was to reach their hearts, he must not only speak their language, but that he must also give the people the Word of God in their own tongue. The Burmans are a reading people, and this was an additional reason for, and a fresh stimulus to, his work. So well did he succeed, that a Burmese governor, who received one of his translations four years after his arrival, could scarcely believe that it was the work of a foreigner. But we cannot dwell on this portion of his work. We may, however, mention here that in 1834, after twenty years of patient toil, he completed his translation of the whole Bible ; and when the last page passed through his hands, he knelt down and prayed " for the forgiveness of Heaven on all the sins that had mingled with his labours, and commended his work to the mercy and grace of God, to be used as an instrument for converting the heathen to Himself." There was then no grammar nor dictionary of the language, and this made his task one of extreme difficulty; but before he died he rendered the work of his successors comparatively light by compiling a grammar, and nearly completing a dictionary of the Burmese tongue. They remain to this day as monuments of his industry and talent, and have not yet been superseded. Nor was this all: he imported a printing press from Serampore, and a printer from America (where the Baptists had adopted his mission), and he published " A Summary of Christian Doctrine," and many valuable tracts, the circulation of which was greatly blessed.

Four years having been spent in preliminary study, Judson went to Chittagong, to try and find amongst the native Christians some one who knew the Burmese tongue, and could assist him in his work. There he was unexpectedly detained for seven months; but his brave wife remained at her post, with other missionaries who had arrived at Rangoon, gathering the native women around her, and teaching them the story of redeeming love. When persecution broke out, she not only prevented the abandonment of the mission by her firmness and decision, but she went in person to the authorities, and by her tact and address obtained a repeal of their harsh enactments. When cholera raged, and the rest of the party resolved to leave for Bengal in the last remaining vessel, she braced her mind to the occasion, returned to the mission house, pursued her studies as formerly, and "left events with God."

On his return Mr. Judson began what he felt to be the great purpose of his life—his evangelistic work. Under the shadow of the grand pagoda, and in a crowded thorough-fare, he built a humble *zayat*, or hall of public resort. Its walls were made of bamboo, and it was covered in with thatch. One room was open to the street, and there he sat all day to receive those whom interest or curiosity induced to listen to his message. Another room was fitted up for public worship, and a third was devoted to classes for the women, and opened on the garden of the mission-house. Quietly and slowly, but steadily and surely, the work went on. Inquirers, opponents, cavillers, found their way to that humble shed. He soon discovered that the philosophies and speculations of Europe had been anticipated in the East; that Idealism and Nihilism had been discussed by Brahmins and Buddhists centuries before the days of Berkeley and Hume; and that amongst the professors of the national creed there existed a large proportion of semi-atheists and metaphysical sceptics. With these he reasoned, dealing now with their common sense, and now with their consciences, pressing home on each the need man has of a Saviour and a Sanctifier, and showing how God has provided these in His glorious Gospel. At length one convert declared himself on the side of Christ, and Moung Nau was baptized as the firstfruits of Burmah unto the Lord. Two others followed; but persecution threatened, and so on a November evening, when the sun had gone down, they made their humble, timid profession. "Perhaps," said the missionary, "if we deny Him not, He will acknowledge us, another day, more publicly than we venture at present to acknowledge Him." It was some comfort to him to find that on the next Lord's-day, after the services were over, "the three converts repaired to the zayat, and held a prayer-meeting of their own accord."

By this time the number of inquirers began to excite the alarm of the Buddhist priests. A new and by no means friendly viceroy had replaced Mya-day-men, who had shown the Judsons no little kindness. He observed the zayat, and it was soon perceived that it was here the converts had learned "to forsake the religion of the country." Moreover the old emperor had died, and his successor, who was supposed to be a zealous Buddhist, had initiated his reign by gilding the great pagoda, which contained the sacred hairs of Gaudama, and by passing sundry enactments in favour of the popular religion. The growing fear of persecution checked inquiry, and the work was likely to cease.

Under these circumstances Judson thought it well to secure, if possible, the royal protection, or, at all events, some measure of toleration, and so he resolved to go to Ava, and to wait upon the emperor. Accordingly, he and Mr. Colman, a brother missionary, set out for the capital, with some valuable presents for members of the court, and a Bible in six volumes, covered with gold-leaf, to lay before the " golden feet." His old friend, Mya-day-men, undertook to present them, and every forehead was laid in the dust as the modern Ahasuerus, with royal gait, and with gold-sheathed sword in hand, gave audience in the splendid palace. After he had asked several questions, and heard the Prime Minister read the petition, he held out his hand for the tract, which contained a brief summary of the Christian faith. As he silently read the opening sentences, the hearts of the missionaries sent up a secret prayer to God—" Have mercy on Burmah ! have mercy on her king ! " But he dashed the paper to the ground with palpable disdain. An attempt to conciliate him was made by unfolding and displaying one of the attractive volumes ; but the " Sovereign of land and sea " took no notice. The Prime Minister interpreted his master's will : —" In regard to the objects of your petition, His Majesty gives no order; in regard to your sacred books, His Majesty has no use for them : take them away."

With a heavy heart they returned home. Before they did so, however, they learned, to their deep dismay, that some fifteen years before a Burmese, who had been converted by the Portuguese priests, and sent to Rome to complete his education, was on his return accused before the authorities by his own nephew, and subjected to the cruel torture of the iron mall. Beaten from head to foot till his body was one living wound, he still pronounced the name of Christ, and refused to deny his faith. The story held out a sad prospect of what converts might expect, but the missionaries gathered some comfort from the sample of constancy which it exhibited ; and strange to say, on their return, the recital of it was blessed in deciding some waverers as to their future course. The missionaries now resolved to leave Burmah for a while, with their three converts, and to go to a region between Bengal and Arracan, where a kindred tongue was spoken. This resolution produced dismay amongst the little group of inquirers at Rangoon. "Do stay with us," they said, "till there are ten disciples, and then appoint one to be the teacher of the rest when you are gone." The appeal was irresistible, and fervent prayer followed it. It reminds us of Abraham's intercession for Sodom; but in this case "the ten" were found. Before five months had passed, Judson was able to take his wife, whose health was seriously impaired, to Calcutta, and to leave the infant church to the native care of Moung Shwa-gnong. But within six months they returned to their little flock, and found their converts, notwithstanding much persecution, true to their profession, and glad beyond measure to welcome them. It was a cheering thing, moreover, to see their old friend, the kindly viceroy, just reinstated in office. The enemies of the Gospel had gone to him with an accusation against the native teacher —"He has turned the priests' rice-pot bottom upwards." "What matter!" said the viceroy; "let the priests turn it back again."

The work went on; disciples began to increase; schools were opened, and two remarkable men, Moung Shwa-ba and Moung Ing, of whom we shall hear again, were added to the Church; so that although "Mama Judson," as the natives loved to call her, was suffering severely from liver complaint, and had to go for two years to America, as her last chance of life, her noble husband resolved to remain at his post. He was almost the only person on earth who had such a knowledge of their language as to be of use to the pagans of Burmah. And so with sorrowful hearts the husband and wife parted. Dr. Price, a medical missionary, now joined the mission. His fame reached "the golden ears," and he was summoned to Ava. Judson accompanied him as interpreter. The reception on this occasion was more favourable than the last; but the " golden mouth " put some alarming questions to Judson: " And you in black, are you a medical man too? " " Not a medical man, but a teacher of religion, your Majesty." " Have any of the Burmese embraced it ? " Judson diplomatically replied, " Not here." " But are there any in Rangoon ? " demanded the emperor. " There are a few." " Are they foreigners ? " persisted the despotic king. Judson trembled for the consequences; but the truth must be told at all hazards. " Some foreigners and some Burmese," he replied. There was an awful silence; but He who is mightier than the kings of the earth restrained man's wrath, and before Judson left the capital he had preached to both king and courtiers, and received an invitation to return and reside at Ava.

Mrs. Judson came back from America in December 1823, with additional missionary helpers, and within seven days of her arrival at Rangoon she and her husband were sailing up the Irrawady, on their way to Ava.

The natives, who had never seen a white woman before, flocked in crowds to witness the wondrous sight, and soon the happy missionary and his devoted wife were installed in the premises assigned them by the king.   Their work in the capital had begun under the most favourable circumstances; he was engaged in preaching, and she in conducting her school, when intelligence arrived of hostilities with the British, followed by the news that Rangoon had been captured! The few Englishmen in Ava were immediately imprisoned, and orders were issued for the arrest of the foreign teachers.   Judson was suddenly seized, in his wife's presence, by an armed band, who threw him on the floor, tied his arms behind his back, and hurried him to prison.   She barred herself with her four Burmese girls into an inner room, to escape the savagery of the infuriated guards.   In the morning she contrived to send the faithful Moung Ing to make inquiries, and he brought back word that Judson and Price and the English merchants were in the death-prison, with three pairs of iron fetters on each, and all fastened to a long pole to prevent their moving.

We cannot enter into the particulars of that two years' terrible captivity, or of the heroic efforts made by Anne Judson to assuage the sufferings of her husband and his fellow-prisoners. But it is not too much to say that it was owing to her tact and intercessions that they were not murdered. It is a record on the one side of the noblest patience, and on the other of the most devoted love. During part of the time, and that too the hottest season of the year, Judson was shut up with some hundred Burmese robbers in a cell that had no window, and they were so jammed together that he could not find room to stretch himself. It was a rare luxury when he obtained the reversion of a lion's cage, after the poor animal had been starved to death, because it was supposed to be mysteriously connected with English power. The head-jailer, himself a branded murderer, was an incarnation of cruelty and mocking jocularity. After a time Mrs. Judson contrived, partly by presents and partly

by appeals, to have the rigour of his bondage somewhat relaxed, and she kept up
secret communications with him by writing
on flat cakes which were concealed in bowls
of rice, and by stuffing scraps of paper into
the mouth of an old coffee-pot.   Only once
during his long captivity did his brave spirit
give way.   His wife had contrived a surprise
that might remind him of home by concoct-
ing something like a mince pie with buffalo
beef and plantains.   He had borne taunts
and insults without shrinking; he had endured fever and ague without dismay; he
had seen some of his European fellow-
prisoners die from extremity of hardship,
and he had not quailed; he had kissed his
new-born baby in his wife's frail arms,
through the iron bars of his cell, and he
had done so without a sigh; but when he
looked upon this touching remembrance of
a happy home and of wifely tenderness, he
bowed his head upon his knees, and the
tears flowed down to the chains that clanked
about his ankles, and the dainty viand
remained untouched.

Mrs. Judson had managed to secrete the manuscripts of his translations in the earth beneath the mission-house; but the rainy season came on, and they were likely to be ruined with the damp. In his dungeon he was anxious about them, and he arranged with her to sew them up in a pillow, so mean in its appearance, and so comfortless withal, that the covetousness of even a Burman jailer should not be excited by it. The little sleep he enjoyed was all the sweeter because his aching head, as well as his anxious heart, was pillowed on the Word of God. When he was sent to another prison-house at Oung-pen-la, which he reached with lacerated and bleeding feet, the ruffian jailers seized for themselves the mat which covered the precious pillow, and threw the apparently useless article away. Moung Ing found the relic, carried it to the mission-house, and by its aid Burmah afterwards obtained the Bible in her native tongue.

When the English advanced upon the capital, Judson was employed by the

Burmese as an interpreter, and sent to the camp to mediate. He discharged the difficult duty so admirably, that he was afterwards thanked by the Governor-General. Sir Archibald Campbell insisted, amongst other terms, upon the release of the Judsons, and they were soon under the protection of the British flag, and on their way to their old station at Rangoon. But most of the converts were scattered, and there was no security for life under Burmese rule; so it was determined to carry the old zayat into the territory recently ceded to the British, and to set up a new mission at Amherst, and subsequently at Moulmein. Here they re-commenced their blessed work, and not without success; but Judson having gone again to Ava in the vain endeavour to obtain religious toleration, returned only to find that his noble wife had died of fever in his absence, and that he was soon to lay his motherless child beside her, under the hopiä (or hope tree), which seemed such a blessed emblem of their rest and resurrection.

Judson was never the same man after

that. He had not indeed lost his holy resolution, but he had lost his cheerful
elasticity. For a time he indulged in an
ascetic spirit, and would live for days alone
amongst the woods, in fasting and prayer,
and seeing only those who came to him for
religious instruction. But he came forth
from this period of seclusion with a new
baptism of energy and devotedness. He
gave up all his patrimony to the cause of
missions, and set out once more to assail the
strongholds of Satan in the old Burman
empire, and especially at Prome, its ancient
capital. He was led to take an especial
interest in the Karens, an interesting and
patriarchal race, who were treated as slaves
by the Burmese, but were infinitely their
superiors in all the better traits of human
character. They had no priesthood, and
scarcely any form of religion, but possessed
strangely truth-like traditions of Paradise,
and the Fall, and the Deluge, and a coming
Deliverer. It was this mission which led him
to know and marry his second wife, Sarah
Boardman, who had shared her first husband's

labours amongst this people while he lived, and was now devoting herself to their best interests after his death. By the year 1836 there were as many as 248 Karen communicants, and the success went on until the converts were reckoned by thousands, and one of the missionaries could say, "Heathenism has fled from these banks; I eat the rice and fruits cultivated by Christian hands, look on the fields of Christians, see no dwellings but those of Christian families."

Eleven years more passed by, and several children were born, but the health of Sarah Judson was shattered by constant toil, and she was ordered, as a last resource, to try a voyage to America. Her husband went with her, intending to see her as far as the Mauritius; but when they reached it, finding that she was fading away, he went on with her to St. Helena, and there she breathed her last on the 1st September, 1845. She had written a beautiful "Farewell," which she meant to give him at parting. It began—

"We part on this green islet, love;
Thou for the Eastern main,

> I for the setting sun, love;
>   Oh! when to meet again?"

and it ended with these invigorating words—

> "Then gird thine armour on, love,
>   Nor faint thou by the way,
>   Till Boodh shall fall, and Burmah's sons
>   Shall own Messiah's sway."

Judson found the lines after she had "gone home," and when he copied them, he wrote after the last verse these words—"'Gird thine armour on'—And so, God willing, I will yet endeavour to do; and while her prostrate form finds repose on the rock of the ocean, and her sanctified spirit enjoys sweeter repose on the bosom of JESUS, let me continue to toil on all my appointed time, until my change, too, shall come."

Judson proceeded to America, but what a change he found since he had left it thirty-four years before! Scarcely one whom he had known was alive to welcome him; but the old apathy about missions had given way to a generous enthusiasm, and he felt pained by the excessive and universal homage that was paid to him. The universities had made him a Doctor by diploma; statesmen and philosophers crowded round him to pay their respects. He was a great man indeed, but the early ambition of his youth was quenched in the deep humility of an aged servant of the Lord. He remained but nine months in the States, and then returned to his work. He had been anxious to find a suitable biographer to write a memoir of his late wife, and was recommended to a lady who had gained no small literary fame under her *nom de plume* of Fanny Forrester. Emily Chubbuck was vivacious as well as talented, and many wondered when they heard that she was to be Dr. Judson's wife; but she made a noble partner for the missionary, and a loving mother to his children. She enriched our literature with one of the most exquisite biographies in the language, and gathered the materials which give us such an insight into the grandeur of her husband's life. Each of Judson's partners had distinctive talents; Anne was a linguist, Sarah a poetess, Emily an authoress. The first had in her most of the heroine, the second most of the missionary, and the third most of the savante. As wives, they were all worthy of such a husband; and he was worthy of them.

The last three years of Judson's glorious life were spent at Moulmein and Rangoon, amidst alternate difficulties and encouragements. An affection of his voice now prevented him from doing much in the way of preaching, but there was the less need of this, as the mission was supplied with other labourers; still he superintended the work, and cheered the workers, and laboured hard himself at his Burmese Dictionary. He had completed the first section of it (the English-Burmese), when weakness, followed by fever, utterly prostrated him, and the physicians prescribed a voyage to the Isle of France. His devoted wife was not in a condition to go with him, but the mission printer and a faithful Bengali servant went in her stead. Four months afterwards she learned the sad news that within a fortnight after she had parted from him he was laid in an ocean grave

(12th April, 1850). "He could not," wrote his widow, "have a more fitting monument than the blue waves which visit every coast; for his warm sympathies went forth to the ends of the earth, and included the whole family of man." He was brave, faithful, patient, hopeful to the end. His last words were uttered in his dear Burman tongue: "It is done." "I am going."

> "Servant of God, well done!
>   Rest from thy lov'd employ;
> The battle fought, the vict'ry won,
>   Enter thy Master's joy.
>
> "The pains of death are past;
>   Labour and sorrow cease;
> And life's long warfare clos'd at last,
>   His soul is found in peace.
>
> "Soldier of Christ, well done!
>   Praise be thy new employ;
> And while eternal ages run
>   Rest in thy Saviour's joy!"

IV.

ON almost any morning in the years 1805 or 1806 a grave and thoughtful young man might have been seen emerging from the gates of St. Bartholomew's Hospital in London, and making his way with rapid steps to his lodgings in Bishopsgate Street. Those who had witnessed his industry and attention in the wards and lecture-room, during the two or three preceding hours, would have concluded that his one object in life was to qualify himself for the profession of a physician. Had they accompanied him to his humble lodging, and seen him shutting his closet door and kneeling down when the clock struck the hour of noon (as was his custom all through life), they would have gathered that he was a pious man. By-and-by, after a hasty meal, the stalwart young pedestrian is on the road to Greenwich, carrying with him a goodly array of mathematical instruments; and if we follow him into the Observatory, we shall find him deep in astronomical studies, and working out difficult stellar problems, under the guidance of the famous Dr. Hutton. Our conclusions as to his ultimate purposes in life have been already somewhat disturbed, and it is difficult as yet to assign the motives which have led him to link medicine and astronomy together in his course of study.

But let us trace his steps as he returns to the metropolis, and makes his way to the reading-room of the British Museum. The librarian evidently knows the visitor, and, without any question asked or answered, furnishes him with writing materials, and with a strange-looking manuscript, which the student begins at once to transcribe. It is in the Chinese character, and contains a Harmony of the Gospels, the Acts of the Apostles, and the Pauline Epistles; the work, as far as can be ascertained, of some Jesuit missionary. Our student spends some patient hours over the precious document, and then once more we find him in his city lodgings.

But now another character appears upon the scene. The small eyes, the high cheek-bones, the peculiar physiognomy, all indicate that he is a Chinaman; while his proud, domineering manner, as he instructs his pupil in the mysteries of his perplexing language, shows at once that he has inherited the characteristics of his race. The Chinese teacher is Yong-Sam-Tak, and his clever, assiduous pupil is Robert Morrison, the embryo missionary, who may lay claim, at least amongst the reformed churches, to be the Apostle of China, and who was destined to give the Word of the living God, in their own peculiar character, to four hundred millions of idolatrous heathen. And now we have obtained the clue to his varied employments, and can explain why his versatile genius has led him to the study of medicine, astronomy, and oriental literature, that he may the better qualify himself for the one great purpose on which he has set his heart.

It is, however, a remarkable circumstance, that, when young Morrison began his study of Chinese, he had not the remotest idea of engaging in missionary work, or that China was to be the scene of his life-long labours. When, on his return to England, after seventeen years of patient toil, he stood in London upon the platform of the Bible Society, with a volume of the Chinese Bible in his hand, a gentleman who addressed the meeting narrated the following story. Many years before, while reading in the British Museum, his attention was attracted to a young man who was studying a book written in strange characters. "I took the liberty," he said, "of asking him what language it was." "The Chinese," he modestly replied. "And do you understand it?" I inquired. "I am trying to do so," was the reply, "but it is attended with singular difficulty." "And what may be your object?" "I can scarcely define my motives," he answered; "all that I know is that my mind is powerfully wrought upon by some strong and indescribable impulse, and if the language be capable of being surmounted by human zeal and perseverance, I mean to make the experiment. What may be the final result, time only can develop. I have as yet no determinate object in contemplation beyond the acquisition of the language itself." Can we doubt that God's mysterious providence was even then, without his knowledge, leading him to, and gradually preparing him for, the great business of his life?

But before we follow him to his distant field of labour, and point out the calm but decided heroism that distinguished him, we must go back a little in his history, and see his antecedents. Though born in Northumberland and spending his early years at Newcastle-upon-Tyne, he sprang from a Scottish stock, and inherited much of the vigour and prudence of his race. His earliest employment was of an humble, kind, and he served his time to his own father as a last and boot-tree maker. From a maternal uncle he obtained the earliest rudiments of an ordinary education, and, except for an excellent memory, and for rigid application, he was not in any way distinguished amongst his companions. He had early given his heart to God, but there was nothing remarkable, as there was in Judson's case, regarding "the rise and progress of religion" in his soul. When he was about one-and-twenty, he made up his mind to enter the ministry of the Scottish Church, and set himself to prepare for it. This led to his admission into Hoxton Academy, better known after its removal as "Highbury College," and here the same characteristics of ardent piety, indefatigable application, and devoted zeal, which marked his after-life, were soon made manifest. It was here, too, he conceived for the first time the idea of becoming a missionary. The preference for this special work did not arise, in his case, from any strong excitement, nor, as far as can be ascertained, from any striking external impulse, but rather from a calm, deliberate view of the state of the heathen, and of his own obligations to his Lord and Saviour. From the beginning of his life to its very end duty was his pole-star, and it was the solemn sense of duty which led him to resolve on being a missionary.

The London Missionary Society had then an academy at Gosport, and to it Morrison was transferred. As yet there was nothing settled as to his field of labour. Mungo Park was then contemplating the formation of a settlement at Timbuctoo, in the heart of Africa, and the young student felt inclined to accompany him; but the burden of his prayers at this time was that "God would station him in that part of the missionary field where the difficulties were the greatest, and, to all human appearance, the most insurmountable." His prayers were heard, and his designation to China was the answer to them. Circumstances had turned the attention of earnest men to that vast country, with its teeming millions of inhabitants. The British and Foreign Bible Society had heard of the manuscript in the British Museum, to which reference has been already made, and it suggested to them the idea of giving the whole Bible to China in its own tongue. But there were serious difficulties in the way. China was closed, not only against the Gospel, but against the commerce of " the outward barbarians." Any open attempt at evangelisation was certain to kindle persecution. And besides all this, the hostility of our own Government to all missionary effort was so decided, that it was hopeless to expect a transit for a Gospel-messenger in a British ship.

But nowithstanding all these obstacles, it was determined to send a missionary to China, and the lot fell on the young student at Gosport. We have already seen how God was preparing him for the work. From the moment that China was assigned as the scene of his labour, he came to London, and gave himself up for two years to those special studies which were most likely to win a way for him amidst a proud and prejudiced, but literary people. Being at length set apart for his work, he sailed for New York, because it was impossible, for the reasons which we have already mentioned, to reach his destination by a direct route. But this was overruled for good. Friends of the truth, in England, furnished him with letters of introduction to others in America, and these again commended him to the American Consul at Canton, and to other men of influence.

A touching incident is on record concerning his stay at the house of a Christian gentleman in New York. Morrison had been taken suddenly ill, and was placed in the gentleman's own chamber, where, in a little crib beside the bed, slept a child, whom it was thought a pity to disturb. On awakening in the morning, she turned to talk as usual to her parents; but, seeing a stranger in their place, was somewhat alarmed. After a moment's pause she fixed her intelligent eyes steadily upon him, and said, "Man, do you pray to God?" "Oh, yes, my dear," said Mr. Morrison, "every day: God is my best friend." The answer seemed at once to reassure the startled child; she laid her little head contentedly upon her pillow, and fell asleep. Morrison often referred to the circumstance, and said that it taught him a lesson of confidence and faith.

As he was about to sail for Canton, and was settling the question of fare and freight with the shipowner, the man of business, looking at him with a smile that only half concealed his contempt, inquired, "Now, Mr. Morrison, do you really expect that you will make an impression on the idolatry of the Chinese empire?" "No, sir," said Morrison, with a dignified sternness, and with a countenance of which it has been said, "it was a book wherein you might read strange things,"—"No, sir, but I expect that GOD will." Those who knew little of him might say that he was too proud to be vain; those who knew him best would say that he was too pious to be proud.

He reached Canton in September 1807, and found himself amongst "the cunning, jealous, inquisitive Chinese." On every side he saw evidence of their worldliness, their ignorance, and their idolatry; and he said to himself, "Oh, what can ever be done with these ignorant, yet shrewd and imposing people ? " " But," he adds, " what were our fathers in Britain ? " Accordingly, he went to work with undaunted heart and unfailing faith. " China," said he, " may seem walled around against the admission of the Word of God ; but we have as good ground to believe that all its bulwarks shall fall before it, as Joshua had respecting the walls of Jericho."

To acquire the language, and to translate the Scriptures into it, were the great objects which he set before him. Evangelistic efforts in the way of preaching must be set aside till the long-closed door was opened for it. The obstacles in his path were enormous. The language itself, both in its spoken and written forms, was confessedly most difficult. There were as yet no grammars to aid him, and, owing to the suspicion of the Government, it was only at the risk of their liberties and lives that teachers could be obtained. His old friend, Yong-Sam-Tak, turned up in China, but was of little use to him. There was as yet but one Englishman, Sir George Staunton, who had made himself master of the language, and though he showed much kindness to the missionary, there were many reasons why, as British representative at Macao, he could not openly render him much assistance. On every side there were jealousies—jealousies between the English and Americans, jealousies between the Company and British Christians; jealousies from the Portuguese Romanists; and, above all, jealousies on the part of "the Celestials," as the Chinese loved to call themselves; and therefore every step had to be taken with the most extreme caution.

For a time he adopted the dress and customs of the Chinese; cut off his hair, and wore a tail; allowed his nails to grow; ate his food with chopsticks; and walked about in a Chinese frock and cumbrous shoes; but he soon found that all this, though he meant it for the best (in his readiness to "become all things to all men"), only awakened suspicion, and that it was wiser to dress like other foreigners who had come for purposes of trade. But he kept on steadily at the study of the language in both the Mandarin and Canton dialects; and with this view procured such books as might assist him; obtained what help he could from native teachers; lived constantly with two Chinese domestics; spoke to them and read to them in their own tongue, and even repeated his private prayers in the language which he sought to conquer. His success may be gathered from the fact that ere long he was appointed translator to the East India Company's factory, a post which, like Carey under similar circumstances, he prized, not so much for the emoluments which it brought with it, as for the facilities it offered for further study, and the opportunity which it gave him to relieve the Missionary Society of expense.

His feelings at this time will be best described in his own words: "But for the cause I serve, I would gladly exchange my present situation for any in England or Scotland at £50 a year. From this barren land I look with mournful pleasure to the fruitful plains of British Israel: your green pastures are plentifully watered by the streams of life; but here, alas! all is cheer-less as the sandy desert. Well, though the prospect now be very, very dreary, we look forward to the time when this barren land shall be turned into streams of water, and the desert blossom as the rose."

We must now follow him to what may be called, both literally and metaphorically, his *subterranean* labours. Privacy, caution, patience, were absolutely necessary for his work. It must be done, if done at all, with the utmost secrecy and consequent self-denial. And so we get a glimpse of the prudent and indefatigable missionary living in a cellar below the roadway, with a dim earthenware lamp lighted before him, and a folio volume of Matthew Henry's Commentary screening the flame both from the wind and from observation. It was a true and real heroism that enabled him to work on day after day, and year after year, for the most part alone, and without any aid from external excitement, or any of those helps which come to us from the countenance and approbation of our fellow-men. He had not even that fuel for

enthusiasm which is to be found in the presence of large and interested audiences, and
which missionaries so often derive, even
from the objections and questionings of their
hearers. Two expressions, which were often
on Morrison's lips, indicated, the one his
strength of motive, the other his source of
strength : the first was, " It is my duty ; "
the second, " Look up, look up."

The first portion of Holy Scripture which
he printed in 1810 was " The Acts of the
Apostles ; " and he always admitted that this
was in effect a revision from the manuscript
which he had studied at home, and which
thus became the nucleus of the Chinese New
Testament. In 1814 he had finished the
rest of the New Testament, and sent it to
the press ; and in the same year he baptized
his first convert, Tsae Ako, who had been
helping him in his work. In 1819, with the
aid of Dr. Milne, the whole Bible was completed, and, by liberal help from the British
and Foreign Bible Society, was published in
twenty-one volumes. During this time he
had to superintend not only the printing,

but also the cutting of the blocks from which the copies were to be struck, and often had his patience and perseverance been tried by finding them destroyed, sometimes by the ravages of the white ants, sometimes through the terror of the workmen, and sometimes through the hostility of the native magistrates. We may add that when he saw imperial edicts issued against Christianity; when his own work was again and again assailed, and for a time interrupted; and even when bitter persecutions were stirred up against his few but faithful converts, this calm and resolute soldier of the cross was not dismayed, but held fast to his convictions and to his duties. When the worldly wisdom of "the Honorable Company" led them to fear that they should be compromised if it were known that their interpreter was engaged in the work of Bible translation, he never for a moment hesitated as to his duty. To use his own words, " The character of a missionary I cannot sink ; no, not if my daily bread depend on it." They went so far as to sever their connection with him for a while; yet, such was their confidence in his wisdom, and their high estimate of his capacity, that he was soon restored to office: they employed him again and again as a Chinese jurist in political matters of the greatest delicacy and importance, and even sent him on one occasion with Lord Amherst on an embassy to Pekin. They also undertook the publication of his Chinese Dictionary, a work which he carried on simultaneously with his Biblical translation. Some idea of the extent and vastness of this work may be formed from the fact that it cost them £15,000 to produce it. It was in reality a Chinese Encyclopædia, explaining some 40,000 characters, and giving a vast amount of information concerning the whole circuit of Chinese literature. We are accustomed to call Dr. Johnson, our English lexicographer, "a Colossus of Literature;" but by what title shall we designate the marvellous compiler of the Chinese Dictionary?

Nor was this his only literary labour. His Grammar of the language; his Chinese

Miscellany; his "View of China for Philological Purposes;" his editing and publish-
ing of the "Notitia Linguæ Sinicæ;" these,
and other works of a similar kind, would
have established for him, as Professor Kidd
has well observed, a world-wide reputation
in the domain of letters.   But we must
remember, as the Professor has also said,
that "whatever he accomplished as an
ardent scholar, a zealous divine, and a
steady patriot, owed its origin to his religious character."

Two special considerations urged him on
in his work of Biblical translation; one was
that both Buddhism and Confucianism had
been mainly spread in the "Flowery Land,"
not by oral teaching or preaching, but by
books; the other was that, although the
dialects of China were manifold (some
reckon them at two hundred), and differed,
many of them, as much from each other as
the languages of Europe, yet the printed
character of the country was intelligible to
all readers.   Perhaps this will be best
understood by an illustration.   The Arabic

numerals (1, 2, 3, 4, etc.), standing as they do, not for sounds, but for numerical notions, are at once understood by all readers, although, as inhabitants of different countries, they will call them by entirely different names. The Chinese written characters, being symbolic, and not phonetic—representing things to the eye, instead of sounds to the ear, are in this way intelligible throughout the empire, and not only there, but in the Corea, Japan, Loo-Choo, and Cochin China, where they are known, and where the press has been in use for seven hundred years. Thus, by translating the Holy Scriptures into the printed characters of China, Morrison provided a book, and that book the Book of God, for one-third of the human family!

It is not pretended that Dr. Morrison's translation of the Bible is a perfect one. It was the first translation into the most difficult language of the world, and it was accomplished under unparalleled difficulties. "The written language of China," says the Rev. A. E. Moule, of Ningpo, " would require almost two lifetimes of unremitting toil." No one knew this better than Morrison himself. He felt the need of a thorough revision of his work, and had his life been spared longer, he would have effected it; but, to use his own words, he studied "fidelity, perspicuity, and simplicity;" and he aimed (it is his own happy illustration) at preparing the way in China, as Wycliffe did in England, for those who should come after him.

His fame as a scholar had reached Europe. French *savants* had corresponded with him. Glasgow had conferred on him the degree of Doctor in Divinity. It was no wonder, therefore, that when he came to England in 1824, after seventeen years of indomitable labour, men like Sir George Staunton, Sir Robert Peel, and Bishop Sumner, should welcome him, and present him to his Sovereign; that his name should be received with cheers in the Imperial Parliament; that literary institutions like the Royal Society should invite him to membership; and that Churchmen and Dissenters should vie with each other to do him honour. His own catholicity of spirit was proved in many ways, and perhaps in none more than in this, that, though a Dissenter, he invariably used the Liturgy of the Church of England in his ministrations to the residents ; and when he wished to bequeath to his native converts a help to their devotions, he translated it into their own tongue. " To me it appeared," he writes, " that the richness of its devotional phraseology, its elevated views of the Deity, and its explicit and full recognition of the work of our Lord Jesus Christ, were so many excellences that a version of them into Chinese, as they were, was better than for me to new model them."

After two years in England, spent, as he says, "mostly in stage coaches and inns "— for he travelled far and near to promote an interest in missionary work—he returned to the land of his adoption, and for the eight years that followed, amidst failing health and family afflictions and manifold discouragements, he still pursued without cessation his multifarious labours. The

Anglo-Chinese college, which he himself had founded at Malacca, and to which he was a most generous benefactor, engaged much of his attention. The printing press was employed not only in printing successive editions of the Holy Scriptures, but also in producing tracts, hymn-books, and catechisms, which were scattered in thousands amongst the population, by means of native Christians and traders, although, as Dr. Morrison truly observes, they seemed " not more in comparison of the vast extent of ground to be cultivated than a handful of seed would be if cast on the mountains of Lebanon." To the Europeans and Americans who resided in Canton and Macao, and to the sailors who visited these ports, he gave religious instruction; but, except to the natives in his own employ, he could give no oral instruction to the heathen, this being rendered impossible by the despotism under which he lived. Still, the few opportunities which he had were diligently employed, and not without success. He did much to raise the tone of morals and religion amongst the foreign residents, and was the means of winning a little band of Chinamen to the profession of Christianity. One of these was Leang Afa, who became the first native preacher of the Gospel in the empire.

Morrison lived to see other labourers arrive in China, and to welcome Dutch and American as well as English missionaries. The work has made vast advances since that "day of small things," but to him belong the credit and the praise of having pioneered the way. We have said enough to show that his talents were of a solid rather than of a showy character, and that the work of missions in China was no less indebted to his caution than to his genius. "One false step at the beginning might have delayed the work for ages."

There was in him, as in many other heroic minds, a strange mixture of the sternest severity in respect to duty, and of the softest affection as regarded those dear to him. His letters to his children, his interest in their sports—nay, the very caresses he bestowed upon his dog "Cæsar," all bear witness to the gentleness of his disposition. His journals breathe a spirit of earnest piety, and at the same time of statesmanlike wisdom. He was generous almost to a fault. As in the cases of Schwartz, Carey, and Marshman, the chief part of his official income was expended upon his missionary work.

He died in harness—"tired *in* the work, but not *of* it"—and he died almost alone; for all but one of his family had gone to England on account of health. He was weak and scarcely able for the effort, but he gathered his little flock of converts round him on the last Lord's day that he spent on earth, and for the last time they heard from his dying lips the clear expression of his faith, the solemn exhortation of his love, and his earnest prayers for them and for his work; and then, on August 1st, 1834, to use the Oriental language of one of that little band, "he entered on his golden tranquillity."

V.

THE missionary heroes whose histories have been already sketched in this volume, found their fields of valour and devotion amongst races which, however benighted, were yet to a great degree civilized, and in some instances positively refined; but we have now to turn to the history of men who spent their lives amidst barbarians, and who won their noblest trophies among cannibals and savages. Foremost of the band stands Samuel Marsden, the "Apostle of New Zealand." This sturdy Yorkshireman, whom no dangers could affright, and whom no difficulties could deter, like many of his fellow-heroes, was born of humble parents, at Horsforth, in the neighbourhood of Leeds, in 1764, and after having received an elementary education in his native village was transferred to the Grammar School of Hull, which was then presided over by Dr. Milner, the well-known ecclesiastical historian. It is said that for a time he worked at the anvil, but that he evinced no ordinary literary promise seems certain from the fact that he was adopted by the " Eland Society," which sought out young men of talent for the ministry, and by it was sent to complete his education at St. John's, Cambridge. This occurred some few years before Henry Martyn became a student at the same college. Before, however, Marsden had taken his degree, the offer of a colonial chaplaincy amongst the convicts of New South Wales was made to him through the influence of Mr. Wilberforce, and on the recommendation of the Rev. Charles Simeon, who had early discovered the peculiar fitness of the young mechanic for a post which was as rough and arduous as it was noble and self-denying. How little did either he or his patrons know for what a destiny God's providence was preparing him ! The youthful chaplain was waiting at Hull, with his newly-wedded bride, for the sailing of the ship which was to carry them to their " distant banishment," when just as he was entering the pulpit on Sunday morning, the signal-gun was fired, and he and his wife had to set out at once for the beach, accompanied by the whole congregation, to whom, instead of a sermon, he gave his parting benediction, and then set sail amidst their prayers and their fare-wells. While the vessel waited at Portsmouth for her cargo of convicts, Marsden visited the Isle of Wight, and it was a sermon of his in Brading Church that led to the conversion of " the Dairyman's Daughter," whose touching story has been so well told by Leigh Richmond in his " Annals of the Poor."

It was a rough and in many respects an unpleasant charge that awaited Marsden at Paramatta. The colony was composed of the worst of felons and bush-rangers—the very scum and refuse of a vicious population who had been banished from their own land for every conceivable crime, and for whose

reformation and instruction scarcely anything had been done. The work allotted to
him was enough to appal the stoutest heart,
but the heroic clergyman entered upon it with
the faith of a man who believed in his
mission, and though he was thwarted and
opposed and misrepresented at every step
by those in authority, he still persevered
" through evil report " (we cannot add " and
through good report ") in carrying out his
own well-laid plans for the benefit of the
abandoned criminals who formed his charge,
and for that of the reckless and brutish
population which surrounded them. It was
the policy, and oftentimes the base self-
interest of those who held power in the colony
to resist all attempts at reformation and
improvement; and as the brave and godly
chaplain persisted in his efforts, he was constantly assailed with personal abuse, official
misrepresentation, and newspaper libels.
Again and again had he to appeal for protection to the laws of his country, and on
each occasion with success; till at last his
philanthropic efforts won the notice and

approbation of such friends of the human race as Lord Gambier, William Wilberforce, and Elizabeth Fry; and better still, his suggestions on behalf of the moral and spiritual welfare of the colony were adopted by the Government at home.

It was during a visit which he paid to England in 1807, for the purpose of laying his plans before the authorities, that he pleaded the cause of New Zealand with the Church Missionary Society, and thus laid the foundation of one of the most remarkable missions of modern times. Fourteen years previously, when on his first voyage to New South Wales, he had read "The Life of Brainerd," and it had kindled in his bosom, as it has kindled in many others, a flame of missionary zeal. Whilst engaged in his projects for the colonists, he did not lose sight of the despised Australian natives, and made frequent though abortive efforts for their good; but his attention was more particularly directed to the New Zealanders. They were feared and hated in New South Wales; but Marsden soon discovered them to be a noble type of savage, though constantly engaged in internecine wars, and often stirred up to murderous reprisals upon white men, by the ill-treatment they received.

They were an inquisitive and enterprising people, and paid frequent visits to New South Wales. Marsden opened his hospitable doors to receive them, and soon gained a wondrous influence over them. Sometimes he had as many as thirty of them beneath his roof. One remarkable chieftain, Tippahee, with his four sons, visited the colony in 1806, and our hero found that the tattooed cannibal was a man of superior ability, anxious for the improvement of his people, and ready to adopt plans for the elevation of his race. Marsden sent him back to New Zealand laden with seeds and tools and useful gifts, and thus prepared the way for the nobler projects which occupied his thoughts.

We can well imagine with what earnestness the vigorous and devoted man of God pleaded the cause of his *protégés* with the committee of the Church Missionary Society in London, and we know with what alacrity they responded to his appeal. No clergymen could at first be found to engage in the heroic enterprise; but two skilled mechanics were placed under Marsden's charge, to visit the islands, to establish friendly relations with the natives, and to use the arts of civilization as a means towards the promulgation of the Gospel. This subordination of means to an end is distinctly marked in their instructions : "Ever bear in mind that the only object of the Society, in sending you to New Zealand, is to introduce the knowledge of Christ among the natives, and in order to this, the arts of civilized life." Whatever may have been Mr. Marsden's earlier ideas with regard to the importance of civilization in its relation to Christianity, his experience, at the end of thirty years of toil, found expression in these words : "Civilization is not necessary before Christianity; do both together if you will, but you will find civilization follow Christianity more easily than Christianity follow civilization." And then he added these memorable words: "I shall not live to see it, but I may hear of it in heaven, that New Zealand, with all its cannibalism and idolatry, will yet set an example of Christianity to some of the nations now before her in civilization." It was this thorough confidence in the truth of God, not only as an end, but as a means, which carried him through hosts of difficulties.

On Marsden's return voyage to Port Jackson, with his two associates, it so happened that a poor, sickly, emaciated New Zealander sailed with them in the same ship. Ruatara, like many of his countrymen, had been cruelly treated by English sailors, who, under delusive promises, had induced him to sail with them to England, and then, after having almost worked him to death, left him in poverty and sickness, to find his way back, as best he could, to his native land. The benevolent chaplain pitied the poor outcast stranger, and inquired into his history. Strange to say, he was nephew to Tippahee; and Marsden soon found that he was endowed with many of his uncle's noblest qualities, and with earnest desires for the advancement of his people. Notwithstanding the cruel treatment he had received, he had been deeply impressed with what he had seen in England, and more especially with the observance of the Lord's-day. The care and tenderness of his bluff but kindly friend soon re-established his health, and won him over to promise his valuable services in aid of Marsden's Christian enterprise.

Upon their arrival at Paramatta, disastrous news awaited them. A large merchantman, the *Boyd*, having put into the harbour of Whangaroa, had been plundered by the natives, and all the passengers and crew had been murdered and devoured. It was afterwards ascertained that the most wanton provocation had been given by the captain to a young chief who had been on board, and hence this horrible retaliation. This, in its turn, led to terrible reprisals. Some whalers, hearing of the loss of the *Boyd*, determined to avenge it, and confounding the innocent with the guilty, came down upon Tippahee in his island home in the Bay of Islands, put him and his people to the sword, and burnt their village to ashes.

The state of excitement was so great that Marsden wisely postponed his missionary enterprise; and meantime Ruatara returned to his home, and began to enlighten his people by recounting what he had heard and seen, by introducing seeds and agriculture, and by "making a Sunday," as he expressed it, for the space of "five moons," at the end of which period he seems to have lost his reckoning, and to have abandoned that part of his plan. At length the two mechanics visited New Zealand, and were joyfully received by Ruatara and his friends, some of whom, in company with the young chief, returned with them to Port Jackson, and filled the anxious heart of the good chaplain with rejoicing, when he saw the near prospect of a commencement for his long-contemplated work.

He could find no captain of a ship adventurous enough to take him and his party to

the land of cannibals. One, indeed, offered
to run the desperate risk; but he asked
£600 for the single venture, and this was
beyond the means at the chaplain's disposal;
so at his own risk he purchased the *Active*,
a little brig, the first of those missionary
vessels which have since done such good
service in the cause of Christ.

On the 19th November, 1814, Marsden
embarked, with a motley crew of Christians
and savages, Europeans and New Zealanders, women and artizans, together with a
few horses, cattle, sheep, and poultry, and
dropped his anchor in the Bay of Islands,
close to the scenes of recent bloodshed and
horror. It was just as the Christmas festival
was drawing near, with its memories of peace
and mercy. The Whangaroans and the
people of the Bay of Islands were still at
war; the one suspected the other of having
conspired with the English in the murder
of Tippahee, and a deadly feud existed
between them. Marsden saw at once that
if he went at first to Ruatara's friends, it
would be misinterpreted by the Whan-

garoans as an act of partiality; so he determined to show that he was the friend of both,
and boldly resolved, not only to land un-
armed amongst the Whangaroans, but, with
only one companion, to spend the night in
their midst.

Perhaps in the annals of heroic enterprise
there never was a braver deed. Ruatara,
who knew the unscrupulous ferocity of his
race, and that they were burning with the
spirit of revenge, did all he could to dissuade the intrepid missionary, but in vain.
A welcome, however, awaited Marsden,
though it was scarcely of a kind to reassure
him. On the hill opposite the landing-
place, a band of naked warriors, armed
with clubs and spears, occupied a command-
ing position. After an anxious pause, a
native advanced, flourishing a red mat, and
crying, "Haromai! haromai!" ("Come
hither! come hither!") Then the warriors
advanced. Some of them wore necklaces
made of the teeth of their slaughtered
enemies; while others were adorned with
the dollars which they had plundered from

the ill-fated strangers whom they had lately murdered on that very beach. Seizing their spears, they brandished them as if in fury. Screams and yells were heard on every side. Every face was fiercely distorted, and every limb employed in the wildest gesticulation. It was their war-dance. "What nearer approach to demons," said Captain Fitzroy, on witnessing one of these performances, "could be made by human beings?" But it was a "*welcome*," for the name of "Marsden," "the friend of the Maories," had reached them through their countrymen who had visited Paramatta.

That night he and Mr. Nicholas remained upon the island. He has described his own sensations:—"The night was clear, the stars shone bright, the sea was smooth; around were the warriors' spears stuck upright in the ground, and groups of natives lay in all directions, like a flock of sheep over the grass, for there were neither tents nor huts to cover them. I viewed our present situation with feelings which I cannot describe—surrounded by cannibals who had devoured our countrymen. I wondered much at the mysteries of Providence, and how these things could be. I did not sleep much; my mind was occupied by the strange circumstances in which we were, and the new and strange ideas which the scene naturally awakened."

As Marsden lay awake that night, there shone above him one of the most striking constellations of the other hemisphere—the southern cross, formed by a group of four brilliant stars. And then there arose another, —the southern crown, that magnificent diadem of light, as if to assure him of the glorious issue of his work, and to cheer him with the remembrance that

> "To patient faith the prize is sure,
> And they, who to the end endure
> The cross, shall wear the crown."

Christmas Day was at hand. It fell upon a Sunday, and Ruatara made preparations for the performance of Divine worship on shore. The English flag was hoisted upon the highest hill above the village in honour of the Christian holiday. About half an acre of ground had been enclosed with a fence; a rude pulpit had been erected, and draped with native mats, and some old canoes turned upside down were arranged as seats for the Europeans. Chiefs and people were gathered all around, while the women and children formed a wider circle outside. A solemn silence prevailed, and then the tones of the grand "Old Hundredth" rose for the first time on that distant shore Marsden entered the pulpit, and preached from the angelic message of the day, "Behold, I bring you glad tidings of great joy." A native who had been on board was the interpreter, and when the people complained that they could not understand it well, Ruatara told them that they would understand it by-and-by, and that he would explain it as far as he could.

Such was the first entrance of the Gospel into New Zealand, and such the heroic man who gained that entrance for it, no less by his kindness than by his courage. From that day onwards, throughout a quarter of a century, he made the mission his constant care.   Residing at Paramatta, and waging there an unceasing war with vice, injustice, and obloquy, his heart was still in New Zealand.   The *Active* passed to and fro continually between Port Jackson and the mission, carrying from time to time fresh labourers to the field, and bringing over young and intelligent natives to be trained under his friendly supervision.   Seven times did this noble-hearted man cross over in his missionary ship, and every time with blessing and advantage to the natives.   At one time it was to set the missionaries to work upon the language, and to compile vocabularies; at another it was to install fresh labourers and mechanics in some new settlement; at another it was to open schools and seminaries for the instruction of the people; at another it was to step in as mediator between hostile tribes, and to stay the fierce ravages of war; always it was to proclaim the Gospel of Christ, and to extend the Redeemer's kingdom.

For a long time there were no converts, and the missionaries were exposed to imminent peril amidst the sanguinary conflicts which surrounded them. But still there was a very general desire amongst the natives that the Pakehas (or Englishmen) should settle amongst them. They were wise enough to see the advantages arising from the presence of civilized and kindly teachers. And on one occasion they earnestly assured Mr. Marsden that there was no danger of the Pakehas being killed and eaten, for " their flesh was not so sweet as Maori flesh, because the English ate too much salt ! " At length a spirit of inquiry was manifested ; the truth of God began to find lodgment in these savage hearts : one chief, and then another, was baptized ; the people followed their example ; houses of prayer sprang up in various directions, and the wilderness began to "blossom as the rose."

When Marsden paid his sixth visit he found a striking contrast on the east and west shores of the bay where he landed. On the one side were naked savages engaged in war ; nothing was to be heard but the firing of musketry, the yells of the combatants, the moans of the wounded, and wild lamentations for the slain. Not one ray of heavenly light or peace upon that dismal shore. On the other, the sound of " the church-going bell; " the natives decently dressed, and assembling for divine worship; the church service printed in their own language, and many of them able to read it, and ready to use it with propriety and devotion. The whole settlement reminded him " of a well-regulated English parish." " Here," wrote the good man, " might be viewed at one glance the blessings of the Christian religion and the miseries of heathenism even with respect to the present life; but when we extend our thoughts to the future, how infinite the difference ! "

His seventh and last visit was a memorable one. He was now seventy-two years of age; he was bowed down with infirmity, and his sight was failing him; but he resolved once more to visit his beloved Maories, in company with his youngest daughter. " The people in the colony," said he, "are becoming too fine for me now. I am too old to preach before them, but I can talk to the New Zealanders." His advent was hailed with unutterable delight. Wherever the venerable patriarch appeared, he was greeted by the native Christians with tears of joy, while the heathen population welcomed him with firing of muskets, and the exhibition of their wardance. One chieftain sat upon the ground, gazing upon him in silence for several hours; and when reproved by a bystander for what seemed like rudeness, he replied, "Let me alone; let me take a last look; I shall never see him again!" At Kaiti, Marsden sat in his arm-chair in the open air before the mission-house, and held a constant levee. Thousands of Maories poured in from every quarter, and from great distances, to do homage to their benefactor. With his characteristic benevolence, he presented each with a pipe and fig of tobacco, and when he was about to re-embark they carried him on their shoulders to the ship, a distance of six miles. With paternal authority, and with all the solemnity of a man who stood on the verge of eternity, the apostolic missionary gave his parting benediction to the missionaries and their native converts, and quitted the shores of New Zealand for the last time.

Amongst the records of the Church Missionary Society has been found a letter from him, written after his return to Paramatta. It is in a large and straggling hand, and dated 10th December, 1837. It was his last communication, and was not received until after his death. In it he writes, "I am happy to say the mission goes on well amidst every difficulty. I visited many places in my last voyage from the North Cape to Cloudy Bay. The Gospel has made a deep impression upon many of the natives, who now lead godly lives." The letter concludes with these touching words: "I am now very feeble; my eyes are dim, and my memory fails me. I have done no duty on the Sabbath for some weeks through weakness. When I review all the way the Lord has led me through this wilderness,

I am constrained to say, '*Bless the Lord, O my soul.*'"

Five months later, on the 8th May, 1838, this grand old man gave up the ghost. He was brave and vigorous to the last. Only a month or two before his death, he and his daughter were stopped by two noted bush-rangers, who presented pistols at their heads, and threatened to shoot them if they spoke a word. Perfectly undismayed, the aged chaplain remonstrated with them on their wicked course of life, and warned them that if they did not abandon it he would probably meet them at the gallows. His words were fulfilled; they were arrested for other outrages, and one of his latest official acts was to attend them to the place of execution!

His last words were spoken in response to a remark on the preciousness of a good hope in Christ—"Precious, precious, precious." And so "the friend of the Maories" and of the convicts died in the presence of all his brethren, having outlived the slander and opposition of all his enemies, and having successfully planted one of the grandest missions of this century. If all who afterwards came into contact with the New Zealand tribes had been actuated by his spirit, the dark shadows which for a time were thrown across this " Britain of the southern hemisphere " had been unknown.

Marsden once entertained the idea that the New Zealand tribes might have been united under one native prince, but he soon found that while every chief was willing to accept the supreme power, not one of them was willing to take a secondary place. He then saw that there was nothing to preserve them from ruin and disintegration, except to bring them under British protection. His last years were employed in preparing them for this event; and two years after his death New Zealand became a British colony, the first, we believe, that was won by her without the sword. At the same time the English episcopate was introduced under the vigorous and benignant sway of the famous Bishop Selwyn. That Episcopate has since been broken up into six different Sees, to meet the growing requirements of the Church; whilst a goodly native ministry and some fifteen thousand native Christians attest the stability of the work, the foundations of which were so well and wisely laid by the heroic " Apostle of New Zealand." It is not too much to say that to Samuel Marsden Great Britain owes, under God, both the colony and the Church of New Zealand.

We shall close this notice of his life and labours by recording the testimony of one who himself may well be claimed as a hero in the mission field. Bishop Selwyn, upon his arrival in the colony, three years after Marsden's death, wrote these memorable words:—" We see here a whole nation of pagans converted to the faith. God has given a new heart and a new spirit to thousands after thousands of our fellow-creatures in this distant quarter of the earth. Young men and maidens, old men and children, all with one heart and with one voice praising God, all offering up daily their morning and evening prayers, all searching the Scriptures to find the way of eternal life, all valuing the Word of God above any other gift, all in greater or less degree bringing forth and visibly displaying in their outward lives some fruits of the influences of the Spirit. Where will you find, throughout the Christian world, more signal manifestations of the presence of that Spirit, or more living evidences of the kingdom of Christ?"

> " His sov'reign mercy has transform'd
>   Their cruelty to love;
> Soften'd the tiger to a lamb,
>   The vulture to a dove!"

VI.

WHAT Cook was amongst navigators, John Williams was amongst missionaries. Both were eminently distinguished for their heroism and for their philanthropy. The lot and labour of both were mainly cast amid those lovely groups of islands, whose feathery palm trees and tufted cocoa-nuts are mirrored in the waters of the Great Pacific. These islands were made known to the civilized world by the one; they were brought into the fellowship of Christendom by the other. Both of these distinguished men lost their lives by murderous hands, upon those distant coasts, in the noble effort to do their duty to God, and to be a blessing to their fellow-men. And if Cook was a real martyr in the cause of science, Williams was a real martyr in the cause of religion.

John Williams was born at Tottenham Court, London, in the year 1796, and gave early evidence of those practical habits which contributed so much to his subsequent usefulness and success. Even as a child, the little breakages of the household were constantly referred to his skill and handicraft for their repair; and when he was apprenticed to an ironmonger in the City Road, it was soon observed that, although exempted by his indentures from the more laborious parts of the business, he preferred the forge to the counter, and became such an expert workman, that he was frequently employed by his master in executing orders which required special skill. He was usually spoken of as "the handy lad;" but no one guessed what valuable results were to flow from his taste and genius for mechanics.

Though brought up by pious parents, he was not religious, and for a time was led into companionships by no means improving to his character. One Sunday evening he was loitering at the corner of a street, waiting for some companions to accompany him to a place of amusement. He was beginning to feel annoyed at their non-appearance, and his natural impatience was increased, because the delay gave occasion to unpleasant self-reflections which were anything but welcome. Just at that moment his master's wife passed by, on her way to " the Tabernacle," and with some difficulty induced the loiterer to go with her. It proved to be the turning-point in his life; and many years afterwards, when, in that same place of worship, the successful missionary was narrating to a breathless audience the story of his labours and successes, " he pointed with deep emotion to the door by which he had entered, and to the pew in which he had sat on that memorable night, when the word of God had been fastened in his heart, as in a sure place, by the Master of assemblies."

The discoveries of Cook had directed the attention of Christian men to the Isles of the Pacific, and the London Missionary Society had selected them as the scene of its earliest labours. These loveliest spots on the earth were becoming depopulated by vice and cruelty. " Mothers slept calmly on the beds beneath which they had buried many of their own murdered infants ! " For many years the early pioneers seemed to toil on in vain. At length there were signs of an awakening. In some of the islands the natives renounced their idolatry, and gave up their bloody rites. There was a cry for help, and when it reached England, Williams was the first to say, " Here am I ; send me."

It was on the 30th of September, 1816, that nine young men stood side by side in Surrey Chapel to receive their missionary designation. John Williams and Robert Moffatt were the two youngest of the band ; the former destined to be " the Apostle of Polynesia," the latter to win for himself, in connection with the dark continent of Africa, a name only second to that of Livingstone, his illustrious son-in-law. The words in which the aged minister who addressed them gave his parting exhortation to John Williams rang not only then, but through all his after life, like a trumpet in his ears: "Go, my dear young brother; and if your tongue cleave to the roof of your mouth, let it be with telling sinners of the love of Jesus Christ; and if your arms drop from your shoulders, let it be with knocking at men's hearts to gain admittance for Him there."

With Mary Chauner, his young and devoted wife, who proved herself a noble helpmeet to a noble husband, Williams and his companions set forth on their missionary voyage. Touching at New Zealand, they received an apostolic greeting from Samuel Marsden, and reached Eimeo, one of the Society Islands, just twelve months after they had left England. Here and in neighbouring islands of the group, Williams remained for some time, perfecting himself in the Tahitian language. He had not the philological powers of a Carey or of a Morrison, nor was he as fruitful as they were in the compilation of grammars and lexicons; neither did he possess the philosophic mind which enabled Judson and Martyn to contend with the sophistries of the East; but he had strong common sense, a marvellous power of endurance, and an extraordinary facility in adapting himself to circumstances; so that by throwing himself thoroughly amongst the simple islanders, he soon got into their habits of thought and expression, while his mechanical skill and unfailing readiness were constant sources of power and influence.

He was led to select Raiatea as the centre of his first missionary operations. It was the largest and most central island of the group; it was moreover the seat of political power, and the head-quarters of idolatry. The temple of Oro, " at once the Mars and the Moloch of the southern seas," stood here, but by a happy accident, or rather by a kindly providence, some knowledge of the Gospel had been already introduced. Pomare, the well-known Christian king of Tahiti, with some of his people and an English missionary, had been driven thither in a storm; and such was the impression made by this unintentional visit, that the chief, whose name was Tamatoa, became desirous that Christian teachers should settle in his island. He came himself to entreat the missionaries to instruct his people. Williams was most anxious to go; but, being the youngest of the band, he waited until all his colleagues had declined the offer, and then joyfully volunteered for the noble service.

There was a grand welcome at Raiatea for "Viriamu;" this being the nearest form of pronunciation that the natives could find in, their speech for the name of "Williams." A present of five pigs for Viriamu, five for his wife, and five for their baby-boy, with abundance of yams and cocoa-nuts and bananas, proved that the people were willing to accept their new teachers. They were ready, moreover, to hear Mr. Williams preach, to observe the Lord's Day, and to renounce their idols; but their moral condition was unutterably debased, their idleness was inveterate, their habits of theft, polygamy, and infanticide were abominable, and their darker and fiercer passions were something awful when roused to war or vengeance.

The story of Mr. Williams' proceedings

and success at Raiatea may be taken as a sample of what he afterwards accomplished at the two other great centres of his vast mission—Rarotonga and Upolu. It would be impossible in a sketch like this to follow him in all his work. An eminent prelate of our Church once compared Mr. Williams' "Narratives of Missionary Enterprise" to the "Acts of the Apostles;" and truly if heroic devotion, consecrated energy, and marvellous results may warrant such a comparison, not one of these elements is wanting. Without for a moment losing sight of his primary work in the evangelization of the people, he employed every art and adjunct of civilization within his reach to raise them from their indolent and brutish habits. He very wisely says in one of his journals, "The missionary does not go to barbarize himself, but to elevate the heathen; not to sink himself to their standard, but to raise them to his." Accordingly, he built himself a house, with window sashes and Venetian blinds, and filled it with neat and commodious furniture, almost every article of

which was made by his own ingenious hands.
He taught the natives how to make lime
from coral, and to build decent houses for
themselves. He set them the example of
gardening and agriculture and boat-building,
and rewarded all attempts at industry by
presents of nails, hinges, and tools.

Soon a place of worship was erected in
their midst, capable of containing some three
thousand people. Williams took care to
make it as far as possible worthy of the purpose for which it was designed. It was truly
a noble Polynesian cathedral, though its
sides were made of wattles, and its pillars of
the trunks of trees. He expended special
care upon the carving of the pulpit and
reading-desk, and fabricated such wondrous
chandeliers for evening service, that when
the natives beheld them they exclaimed,
" Au Brittanue e! Au Brittanue e!" "O
England, O England!" "A Fenua maraau
ore;" "the land whose customs have no
end."

These were, however, but means towards
an end, and that end was the salvation of

souls and the extension of the Redeemer's kingdom. Christianity began to make its way. The maraes, or idol houses, were pulled down; the gods were committed to the flames, infanticide was abolished, cannibalism had ceased, divine service was held three times every Sunday, family prayer was universal, and the people who lately seemed as if possessed by devils were "sitting, and clothed, and in their right mind." "With respect to civilization," says Mr. Williams, "we have pleasure in saying that the natives are doing all that we can reasonably expect, and every person is now daily and busily employed from morning till night. At present there is a range of three miles along the sea-beach studded with little plastered and whitewashed cottages, with their own schooner lying at anchor near them. All this forms such a contrast to the view we had here three years ago, when, excepting three hovels, all was a wilderness, that we cannot but be thankful, and, when we consider all things, exceedingly thankful for what God has wrought."

Williams was a statesman as well as a mechanic. In May 1820 he succeeded in getting a new and admirable code of laws established in a great assembly by the votes of the people. Trial by jury was a distinctive feature of this code, and such an efficient executive was provided from amongst the natives themselves, that the whole system worked admirably. He laid the foundations, moreover, for a remunerative commerce, by teaching them how to cultivate cotton and tobacco, as well as by instructing them in rope-making and other useful arts. He taught them how to prepare the sugar-cane for the market, and not only constructed a mill for the purpose, but made with his own hands the lathe in which the rollers for it were turned.

It was both a test of his work and a proof of its real progress, when he proposed to the converted islanders the formation, amongst themselves, of a Missionary Association for the evangelization of the heathen in the surrounding islands. The speeches that were delivered, and the interest that was evinced by them in reference to this work, but above all the contributions that were given towards carrying it on, proved how deeply the truth of God had taken root in their own hearts. At the end of the first year the Raiateans had given some 15,000 bamboos of cocoa-nut oil, the value of which was at least £500, as a recognition of their own obligations to the Gospel, and of their earnest desire to make it known to others.

The ardent spirit of Williams was not to be restrained within the boundaries of Raiatea. He longed to branch out into the regions beyond. From time to time he heard amongst the natives strange songs and traditions of an island which they called Rarotonga, and all he heard concerning it made him anxious to discover it, and make it the centre of another missionary effort. It so happened in God's providence that, while he was meditating on the subject, some natives from this then unknown island arrived at the missionary settlement, and confirmed his resolution. "I cannot," he said, "content myself with the narrow limits

of a single reef; and if means are not provided, a continent would be to me infinitely
preferable; for there, if you cannot ride, you
can walk; but to these isolated islands a
ship must carry you." Year after year he
appealed to Christians in England to enable
him to procure a vessel wherewith to carry
out his heroic purpose, but his appeals
proved fruitless. At length, undertaking a
serious pecuniary responsibility, he procured
a schooner called the *Endeavour*, and, with
some native Christians and the Rarotongan
visitors, set out upon his voyage of discovery. The story reads like a romance,
and reminds one of Columbus and his search
for the new world. Baffled day after day in
his efforts to discover the traditionary island,
he still persevered. The provisions were all
but exhausted; the captain came to the
missionary early one morning, and said to
him, "We must give up the search, or we
shall all be starved." Williams begged him
to steer on until eight o'clock, and promised
that if the island were not then in sight he
would return home. It was an anxious hour.

Four times had a native been sent to the top of the mast, and he was now ascending for the fifth. Only half-an-hour of the time agreed upon remained unexpired, when suddenly the cloud-mist rolled away, the majestic hills of Rarotonga, the chief of the Hervey group, stood full in view, and the excited sailor shouted, "Teie, teie, taua fenua nei!" "Here, here is the land we have been seeking!"

It would occupy more space than we can spare, to tell how the story of Raiatea was repeated at Rarotonga, and how, within twelve months of its discovery, the whole population, numbering some seven thousand, had renounced idolatry, and were engaged in erecting a place of worship, six hundred feet in length, to accommodate the overwhelming congregations.

But not even triumphs like these could satisfy the grand aspirations of this devoted man. He looked out upon the vast Polynesian world of islands which still remained unevangelized around him and beyond him, and he resolved to build a ship of his own, in which he might roam through the vast Archipelago of the western world. His account of the building of that ship reads like another romance, and has been compared to a chapter in De Foe; but while it equals that story in interest, it has the great advantage of reality. With none to help him but the natives whom he had raised from savagedom; with only a few rude tools, and with no experience save that which he had acquired as an ironmonger's apprentice, he planned and carried to completion his ambitious project. The natives looked on in wonder as the teacher built his ship. One day, when he had forgotten his square, he wrote for it to his wife, upon a chip, which he told a chief to carry to Mrs. Williams. "What shall I say?" inquired the puzzled Rarotongan. "Nothing," replied the missionary, "the chip will tell her;" and when, on reading the message, she gave him the square, the astonished chieftain ran through the settlement, exclaiming, "Oh! the wisdom of these English! they make chips talk!" and he tied a string to the mysterious missive and hung it as an amulet around his neck!

The story of his bellows is well known. There were only four goats on the island, and three of them were killed to furnish the leather for it. But during the night the rats of Rarotonga, which were like one of the plagues of Egypt, congregated in vast numbers, and left nothing of the bellows except the boards. Williams then ingeniously constructed a blowing machine, on the principle of the common pump, which defied the rats, and accomplished his purpose. And then the builder was soon on board his "Messenger of Peace," which the natives called "the Ship of God," and was carrying the glad tidings of the Gospel to the surrounding shores.

And this led to the establishment of his third, and perhaps most interesting station, in the Samoan or Navigator's group. Less superstitious and more intelligent than the inhabitants of the Hervey or Society Islands, the Samoans were even more ready to receive the Gospel. In some instances converts from the other islands had prepared them for the missionary; and he was met by the joyful greeting, "We are the sons of the Word!" In others, the fame of "the wonderful white man" had preceded him, and secured a hearty welcome. His progess was like that of a conqueror, and wherever he went preaching the Gospel of God's grace, the thronging multitudes flocked to him "as doves to their windows," until out of 60,000 some 50,000 were under instruction. His visits to the surrounding islands were looked for with most intense anxiety, and song and dance bore witness to the influence which he exercised, and to the affection in which he was held. One of these Samoan ballads has been happily preserved:

<blockquote>
" Let us talk of Viriamu.
Let cocoa-nuts grow for him in peace for months.
When strong the east winds blow, our hearts forget him not.
Let us greatly love the Christian land of the great white chief.
All victors are we now, for we all have one God!
No food is sacred now. All kinds of fish we catch and eat,
Even the sting-ray.
</blockquote>

> " The birds are crying for Viriamu,
> His ship has sailed another way.
> The birds are crying for Viriamu,
> Long time is he in coming.
> Will he ever come again ?
> Will he ever come again ? "

We doubt whether, since the days of the Apostles, any one man was the means of winning so many thousands to the true faith of Christ by the preaching of the gospel; and he has left this striking testimony concerning his work : " Having witnessed the introduction of Christianity into a greater number of islands than any other missionary, I can safely affirm that in no single instance has the civil power been employed in its propagation." And again, having noticed the moral influence of the converted chieftains upon their people, he says: " Christianity has triumphed, not by human authority, but by its own moral power, by the light which it spread abroad, and by the benevolent spirit which it disseminated; for *kindness is the key to the human heart*, whether it be that of savage or civilized man ; and when, instead of being barbarously murdered, they were treated with kindness, the multitude immediately embraced the truth, for they naturally attributed the mighty transformation in these formerly sanguinary chieftains to the benign influence of the Gospel upon their minds."

Eighteen years had now been spent in labours such as these. Several helpers had come out to aid him, and he had located them along with native teachers in several leading stations, so that he could say, " There is not an island of importance within two thousand miles of Tahiti to which the glad tidings of salvation have not been conveyed." But a vast work remained still to be accomplished. New Caledonia, the New Hebrides, and, farther off, New Guinea, with their countless multitudes, lay in darkness. " The harvest was plenteous, but the labourers were few ; " and so he resolved to visit England, in order to tell of the 300,000 savages already brought under Christian instruction; to get his Rarotongan version of the Scriptures through the press ; and to beseech his countrymen to come " to the help of the Lord against the mighty."

He reached London in 1834, and it is not too much to say that this visit did more to fan the flame of missionary interest than any event which had occurred for a century. When, at the end of four years, he sailed down the Thames in the *Camden* (a vessel of 200 tons burden, which had been expressly purchased for his use, at a cost of £2,600), he was accompanied on his voyage by sixteen other missionaries and their wives, and was followed by such a gale of prayer and sympathy from the tens of thousands who had been thrilled by his narratives, as plainly testified how much his visit had been blessed to hearts at home.

Visiting in turn all his old stations, he planted schools in some, and left fresh labourers in others, and soon we find him at the Samoas again; where, fixing upon Upolu as his home, and making it the third and as it proved the last centre of his evangelistic achievements, he yearned over the benighted islands that still lay beyond him in " the shadow of death." Erromanga was the key to the New Hebrides, and they in their turn to the Papuan races of New Guinea; and so he set his heart upon Erromanga; though, with a strange and unaccountable foreboding, his wife endeavoured to extract a promise from him that he would not land upon its shores. His last Sunday amongst the Samoans seemed wrapt in gloom. The sorrow of his people on parting from him was intense; his own previsions were distinct as to the difficulties of dealing with a race who were known to be violent and suspicious, and who had been frequently exasperated by the cruelties of the white men, who visited their coasts from time to time in search of sandal-wood; all these things pressed upon his heart, naturally buoyant though it was, and probably led him to select the Apostle's text at Miletus for his last address: "They all wept sore, and fell upon Paul's neck, and kissed him; sorrowing most of all for the words which he spake, that they should see his face no more."

On the 20th November, 1839, Dillon's

Bay was reached, and a party from the ship visited the shore. The natives showed no hostile attitude, but were shy and sullen, and it was observed that all the women were kept out of sight. Although this created some suspicion, still the presence of several children at play removed it. Mr. Williams was the second of the little band of four who landed. He offered his hand to the natives, but they declined it; he then presented some cloth, which they accepted. He was engaged in enlisting the attention of the children, when a cry of "danger" from the boats caused all the party to run. The captain and a Mr. Cunningham escaped. Mr. Harris, who had been foremost in the advance, was killed at once; and just as our missionary hero reached the beach, and was almost out of danger, he stumbled in the surf. A heavy blow from a club felled him in the water; it was repeated again and again as he regained his feet; and a whole flight of arrows speedily completed the dreadful tragedy.

So fell the martyr of Erromanga, at the

early age of forty-three, but not until he had accomplished a work which has made his name immortal. The last words he ever wrote, and which were left unfinished in his memorandum-book but a few hours before his death, have a prophetic ring about them :—

" This is a most memorable day, a day which will be transmitted to posterity; and the record of events which have this day happened will last long after those who have taken an active part in them shall have retired into the shades of oblivion; and the results of this day will be——"

There can be little doubt that the horrid orgies of cannibalism followed closely upon the murder; for when H.M.S. *Favourite* visited the island to recover the bodies, a few bones were given up as the only remains of the man who had done so much good in his day and generation. These were carried to Upolu, and laid beside his desolate home and widowed church. The noblest monument that could be raised to his memory was the resolution of his Samoan converts to carry on that work, in the pursuit of which their beloved teacher fell, and to plant the standard of the cross upon the soil of Erromanga.

Again and again they attempted it at the peril of their lives; but each repulse only led to fresh endeavours, which at length were crowned with success. Dr. Selwyn, the Bishop of New Zealand, contributed in no small degree to this blessed result. On his first visit to the New Hebrides he touched at Erromanga with a native teacher. They knelt together on its blood-stained shore, and asked God to open a way for His Gospel to the degraded inhabitants. He brought some of the natives with him to New Zealand, instructed them in the Word of God, and sent them back to their country-men to create a more favourable impression concerning white men than prevailed at the period which we have just described. At length, in 1852, two native Christians from the Hervey Islands were landed, and one of those chiefs who were most forward in giving them a welcome was the very man who had murdered Williams. It turned out upon inquiry that some foreigners had killed his own son, and that he had avenged himself upon the first white man who came within his reach; but the very club which struck the fatal blow was surrendered to the missionaries, and the prayer which had been offered up on that ensanguined beach was at length fully answered.

Erromanga, however, was to have other associations with the noble army of martyrs before that blessed consummation could be attained. In 1861, Mr. and Mrs. Gordon, a devoted missionary pair, were savagely massacred by some of the heathen. It is a touching link between two other martyrdoms and theirs, that they were buried close to the spot where Williams fell, and that the funeral service of the Church of England was read over their graves by Bishop Patteson, who was himself destined to become " the Martyr of Melanesia."

The deaths of these eminent Missionaries have contributed, more perhaps than did their devoted lives, to awaken a spirit of sympathy with their work, and to inspire a belief in its reality. They show that the spirit of self-sacrifice is not extinct in the Church of God, and that as in Apostolic times, so now, there are those who "count not their lives dear unto themselves," so that they "may finish their course with joy," and bear the glad tidings of salvation unto the very ends of the earth.

> "They climbed the steep ascent of heav'n
>   Through peril, toil, and pain;
> O God, to us may grace be giv'n
>   To follow in their train!"

VII.

WILLIAM AUGUSTINE BERNARD JOHNSON.
WEST AFRICA. 1816—1823.

THE name that stands at the head of this chapter is not so well known as those which have preceded it in these sketches; but it is no less entitled to a place beside them, and deserves to be better known, both on account of the personal character of the man who bore it, and of the marvellous work which he was permitted to accomplish.

The same year that saw Williams going forth to Polynesia beheld Johnson going forth to Western Africa. The fields were in many respects utterly unlike, and the characteristics of the men were widely different. The isles of the Pacific, notwithstanding all their beauty and fertility, were inhabited by races distinguished for their vice and ferocity; they needed a conqueror and a civilizer, and they found one in Williams. Africa, darkened by devil-worship, and crushed and brutalized by the slave-trade, required an emancipator and a " son of consolation," and she found both in Johnson. Each was admirably suited for the work which God had given him to do ; and though the former laboured for more than twenty years, and the latter for less than seven, the successes which they individually achieved will endure comparison.

Johnson was by birth a Hanoverian, and had passed a few years in a German counting-house; but when the call to missionary labour reached him at the age of twenty-eight, he filled the very humble position of workman in a sugar-refiner's establishment at Whitechapel in London. The story of his own conversion, which had happened three years previously, was a remarkable one. It was war-time; his wages were scanty; provisions were dear; his wife and himself were on the brink of starvation; and the poor labourer was brought down to the very verge of despair. He had come home one evening utterly hopeless, and with scarcely raiment to cover him ; there was no food in the house ; his wife was weeping ; he threw himself upon the bed beside her, and tossed to and fro in an agony of woe— "No friend to go to." "What to do I did not know."

Just then the remembrance of a verse which he had learned when only eight years old flashed across his mind. It had been impressed upon him in a curious way. The schoolmaster expected every child to repeat on Monday morning some portion of the sermon which had been preached on the previous Sunday. On one occasion the only part that William Johnson could remember was the verse, "Call upon me in the day of trouble, I will deliver thee, and thou shalt glorify Me." As it was only a text, the schoolmaster did not consider it sufficient, and expressed his dissatisfaction with his young pupil. This grieved the boy exceedingly, but it had the effect of impressing the passage indelibly upon his mind. And so in the anguish of his soul that verse came back to the despairing man. "Call upon Me!" But will He hear me if I call? Have I not sinned against Him? Oh, what shall I do? no worldly prospects, and an angry God! He passed a wretched night; went early to his work; came back to his home at what to other men was breakfast-hour, but came, because to stay behind would only have awakened suspicion as to his misery. His wife met him at the door with a joyous smile; she had obtained unexpected employment, and wages in advance, and his breakfast was ready. "My feelings at that moment," he afterwards wrote, "I cannot well express. The greatest sinner in the world, and God so merciful!" He remembered that there was an evening service in the German church at the Savoy, and he resolved to go to it. A Moravian missionary preached, and that sermon brought him to Christ.

From that moment he longed to bring others to the same Saviour. His wife was the first object of his solicitude, and though at first she resisted his endeavours and entreaties, she was eventually given to his prayers, and afterwards became his willing and devoted helper in his work. He attended Bible and missionary meetings, and on one occasion was present when three young men were dismissed to their distant field of labour. As one of these opened his heart, and told how he had been led to think of engaging in missionary work, Johnson's heart was stirred: he thought of the misery of the heathen; of all that Christ had done for himself, and he felt as if he too must go. His own words are remarkable. "These were my feelings that night: I was drowned in tears; I turned myself to the wall, and gave free course to the feelings of my heart. In this state was my mind for some time. "Oh, if I could but go! here am I, O Lord, send me." There were, however, many difficulties in the way, and he tried to quench the new-born desire. This led to coldness and darkness and carelessness. Another address from the pulpit aroused him. "Are any of you in darkness?" said the preacher, "examine yourselves; for something is the reason that God hides His face." Johnson examined himself, and the issue was that he was constrained to cry, "That is it! that is it! Lord, to Thee nothing is impossible. Here am I, send me if it is Thy will."

He who had put the desire into his heart soon opened the way for its accomplishment. A countryman of his own, Henry Düring, had been accepted by the Church Missionary Society as a schoolmaster for Sierra Leone. He called on Johnson, and told him that they wished to send another with him in a like capacity. The case was laid before the fathers of that Society, and they at once accepted him. And so these two men went forth in the same ship (1816), were afterwards ordained together on the same day, and the one at Regent's-Town and the other at Gloucester wrought such a wondrous work for God in Africa as more than justified the Society in its choice, and laid the foundation of those native churches which are now the hope and glory of that dark continent.

But we must now turn to the state of

things at Sierra Leone, in order to understand the work which lay before our missionary. This peninsula on the western
coast of Africa had been discovered by the
Portuguese, and from them received its
name, which means "the Mountain of Lions."
It had been the theatre of some of the
darkest, as it was to become that of some of
the brightest, scenes in that strange land.
Here, as at various other places along the
coast, the slave-trade had been perpetrating
its cruelties, and pushing its horrid trade in
human flesh and blood. The native chiefs
were induced by the offers of enormous
profits to engage in this accursed traffic;
and white men, calling themselves Christians,
were those who held out the tempting bribe,
and then consummated their wickedness by
carrying off the wretched victims of their
avarice into distant lands, to pine and die
beneath the lash of their task-masters.

The captives taken, some of them in midnight expeditions, and others in cruel wars,
were chained together, and driven in gangs
to the sea-board, where they were secured

in barracoons until the slave-ships arrived in sight. Sad and dreadful were the scenes to be witnessed inside and around those horrid enclosures. Here you might see a melancholy procession of forty or fifty negro girls, advancing with bleeding feet, and all bound together by an iron chain passed through the collars which clasped their necks. There you might behold a gang of sorrowful men, fastened together in pairs, and driven along, with oaths and curses, to their terrible prison-house. From within might be heard the wail of miserable mothers, whose children had been torn from them, or whose infants had been put to death ; and often amidst these agonizing cries there arose the groans of the dying, whose sufferings and exhaustion were about to release them from the miseries of life.

By-and-by the slave-ship is in sight, and the wretched captives are transferred to the care of the hardened slave-dealers on board. Who can picture the horrors of that "middle passage" ? Imagine four hundred miserable beings crammed into a hold that was only twelve yards long, by seven wide, and three and a half high! Packed "like herrings in a barrel;" stifled with the suffocating heat; kicked and beaten when they ventured to complain, and scantily supplied with food to eat, or still worse, left without any water with which to quench their thirst! No marvel that scarcely three out of every ten reached their destination, and that many of the survivors were so broken down in constitution that it was more economical for their new proprietors to "use them up," and to purchase fresh slaves, than to give them such nourishment and medicine as might prolong their lives.

But the spirit of Christianity at length put forth its power. The voices of Sharp, and Thornton, and Clarkson, and Wilberforce pleaded the cause of humanity and religion. English judges declared that slaves could not live on British ground, and that the moment they touched it they were free. England awakened to a sense of her sin and of her responsibility. At an enormous cost, the nation emancipated the bondsmen in her own colonies, and then took measures to check the African slave-trade. With a view to this, our squadrons watched the coast, pursued the slave-ships, and liberated the captives on the shores of their own land.

But the efforts of Christian men did not cease with the political emancipation of the slave. There was yet a higher liberty to be achieved. The charter of missionary effort ran thus: " Ye shall know the truth, and the truth shall make you free," and British Christians resolved to extend that freedom to the down-trodden sons of Ham. By a concurrence of providential circumstances Sierra Leone became the place where this noble enterprise was to be put into execution. Thither the English cruisers brought the manumitted slaves, and by a happy arrangement, entered into between the British Government and our missionaries, placed them under Christian instruction. Among these emancipated Africans were to be found the representatives of numerous tribes in the interior, and samples of 150 different dialects have been collected together from the Queen's Yard at Sierra Leone. Thus marvellously had the providence of God overruled the cruelties of the slave-trade to accomplish purposes of Divine mercy, and to bring whole races within the reach of missionary influences.

It was to labour amongst these poor negroes that Johnson went forth. The sainted Edward Bickersteth had preceded him to the colony to make arrangements, and on the arrival of our missionary, placed him at Hogbrook, better known in after days as Regent's-Town, to take the charge and education of some 1,500 of these miserable negroes. I call them miserable, for the iron had indeed entered into their soul. Emaciated by hunger, and ulcerated with disease, they were dying at the rate of seven or eight a day, and those who were fortunate enough to survive were degraded in mind as well as in body. Johnson felt deeply depressed, and the more so because, notwithstanding all his kindness to them, his wretched protégés seemed callous and indifferent. Sunday came, and, to his mortification, only nine attended, and these were almost naked. The truth was, they had suffered so much at the hands of white men that they were still suspicious of their intentions. But Johnson persevered. He had to dole out their daily allowance of rice, and he took advantage of every opportunity to show them sympathy and consideration. This soon began to tell. The Sunday congregations overflowed his cottage, and had to assemble in a large shed, and thence to move into the open air. His school was thronged; but how was he to teach it? His pupils had never seen a book, or known a letter. He selected twelve boys, and taught them the first four letters of the alphabet. He then divided his school into twelve classes, and made each boy teach a class. He next taught his swarthy pupil teachers four letters more; these communicated their knowledge to the rest, and so by degrees the whole alphabet was mastered. Before twelve months had passed, some of his scholars were reading the New Testament.

But Johnson was not content with his success as a schoolmaster. His heart yearned over his charge, and he laboured to raise them from their spiritual bondage and degradation. Happily his journals are preserved, and they give us some idea of his unceasing and prayerful labours as an evangelist. He had been set apart for the ministry by the Lutheran missionaries, but his work had to be carried on amidst great and manifold difficulties. The climate was deadly in the extreme; the fellow-helpers who came out to him were constantly dropping and dying at his side. The crowded graveyard at Kissy is to this day a memorial of the dauntless bravery of that heroic band who formed the forlorn hope of Africa. He was himself frequently prostrated by fever; his noble wife was bearing up against bad health and privations; and at the end of three years he had to take her to England in order to save her life.

But what was the record which he was able to give concerning those three years of devoted labour? He could tell of an organized and Christian community, living together in a well-laid-out and well-built town of their own construction, with a church capable of containing 1,300 people, and filled to overflowing, three times on each Lord's-day, with attentive congregations. He could speak of 263 communicants; of a daily service at which never less than 500, and sometimes as many as 900, attended; and best of all, of real conversion unto God, and of visible and undeniable proofs thereof in the altered life and conduct of his people.

An aged and honoured missionary lately informed me, that when Johnson visited England (1819), he told him that the first evidence of a real impression having been made upon the native mind presented itself at a time when his own heart was overpowered by his apparent want of success, and when he was ready to surrender his work in utter despair. He had wandered into the dark forest, and sat down to meditate and mourn, when suddenly he heard a native voice from amongst the thick bushes breathing forth the heart's anxieties in earnest prayer to God. It was a " token for good," and the missionary went back to his labour strengthened and comforted, to meet from day to day with fresh and increasing proofs that his " labour was not in vain in the Lord."

The following is an extract from a report sent home to the British Government by the authorities at Sierra Leone :—

" Let it be considered that not more than a few years have passed since the greater number of Mr. Johnson's population were taken out of the holds of slave-ships; and who can compare their present condition with that from which they were rescued, without seeing manifest cause to exclaim, ' The hand of Heaven is in this!' Who can contrast the simple and sincere Christian worship which precedes and follows their daily labours with the grovelling and malignant superstitions of their original state, their greegrees, their red-water, their witchcraft, and their devil-houses, without feeling and acknowledging a miracle of

good, which the immediate interposition of
the Almighty alone could have wrought?
And what greater blessing could man or
nation desire or enjoy, than to have been
made the instruments of conferring such
sublime benefits on the most abject of the
human race?"

Nothing strikes one more, in reading the
records of West African missions, than the
childlike simplicity of the people's faith, and
the intense earnestness of their devotions.
Johnson records many of their prayers. We
give one which in its broken English and
deep intensity may be taken as a sample of
the rest. The missionary was standing outside his schoolroom window, and overheard
a scholar praying thus: "O Lord, we have
been so long on the way to hell, and we
have no been saved; we been hear your
good word so long, and we been no consider.
O learn us how to follow you now. We live
nigh hell. O Lord Jesus, save us, save us!
We want you to do it now—now we want
you to save us. O Lord Jesus, hear us this
night! our sins too much; O save us—save

us." No wonder that the pious missionary should add, "I could stay no longer, but went home. My heart was full; I gave free course to the fulness of it. I was drowned in tears. O my God and Saviour, what hast Thou done! What shall I render unto Thee?"

The negroes were, as may be gathered from the foregoing, an excitable people, and it needed great wisdom on Johnson's part to keep their enthusiasm within bounds, and to distinguish between what was real and what was only emotional in their impressions. Indeed, he had in this respect to contend with two opposite influences. The Governor, who seemed to look upon baptism as a sort of political ordinance by which Africans were to be converted into Englishmen, was continually urging our missionary to admit all comers into the Church; whilst one of the timid native catechists, whom Johnson designates as "that fearful Tamba," was so full of apprehension lest any hypocrite should gain an entrance, that he was continually raising objections against the administration of the rite. Johnson, however, steered a middle course, and the best evidence of his wisdom in so doing may be found in the fact that, after the lapse of many years, and notwithstanding many hindrances and discouragements, the church and congregation which he founded at Regent's-Town had maintained its early character for piety and stability.

The love that was felt towards him by his people might be judged of by their sorrow when he left them in order to take his wife to England. They accompanied him in hundreds on foot to Freetown, a distance of some five miles; and when they could go no farther, they pointed to the sea, and exclaimed, "Massa, suppose no water live here—we go with you all de way—till feet no more." And he reciprocated their affection: "Had I ten thousand lives," he says, "I would willingly offer them up for the sake of one poor negro;" and when, at the close of 1819, after his brief six months' visit to England, he was re-embarking for Africa, he observes, "The climate, it is true, is still very unhealthy; and some of my dearest friends and brethren in the Lord have fallen victims to it since my departure. But by the grace of God, none of these things move me. I am ready to go to Sierra Leone, and die for the name of the Lord Jesus." We may add that a devoted sister, whom he had won to Christ, accompanied him and Mrs. Johnson on their return to Africa.

The joy and excitement evoked by his return is best told in the language of a native teacher: " In the evening Mr. Wilhelm keep service. . . . When he done praying, and the people begin to go out, one man come into the church, and said, ' All people hear! Mr. Johnson send me to come and tell you—he *come!* he live in the town!' And the people begin to make a noise. Some could not get out through the door, but jumped out through the window—they so full of joy. Some went to Freetown the same night; and some sing all the night through."

Once more we find him in active work; correcting mistakes which had arisen in his

absence through the indiscretion of his representatives; building up the native church
in steadiness and godliness; advancing the
natives by means of agriculture and fisheries
and public works; raising the schools to
progress and efficiency, and above all making
Christ known to sinners as the one way of
life and salvation. Nor did Johnson confine
his regards to Regent's-Town. He had
early conceived plans for the vast interior of
Africa. "Ah!" he writes, "how far are
our thoughts from those beyond the colony,
just as if there were no other heathen in
Africa! . . . For my part, I feel just like a
bird in a cage. . . . My mind is wandering
into the interior of Africa. Is this mere
imagination? . . . Lord, hast Thou designed
me to proceed from hence into other parts of
Africa? Here am I, send me." And so
we find him again and again making missionary explorations, amidst much hardship
and peril, now all around the peninsula of
Sierra Leone, and again in company with
native Christians (one of them being a Henry
Martyn!) to the Bananas, where we find him

holding palavers with the natives amidst their greegrees and devil-houses.

In 1822, the returning and increasing illness of his wife necessitated the pain of parting from her, and of sending her to England; but for a year longer he laboured on alone amidst mingled joys and sorrows, successes and discouragements. His work was nearly done, though he knew it not. Ophthalmia had broken out in the colony, and he suffered severely from it. His general health was manifestly affected; his throat showed palpably that he needed rest, and the doctors urged him to take it. His wife was recovering, and he longed to bring her back to labour with him again. And so he sailed for England in April 1823. In his last report, written a few weeks before he left Regent's-Town, he could speak of 1,079 scholars, of whom 710 could read; he could tell of his 450 communicants; he could rejoice over his prosperous Missionary Association, and the liberality of his people's contributions to it; he could write about the general progress of industry and civilization in the district; and, above all, concerning the increase and deepening of spiritual life amongst his converts.

He hoped to come back to his work again; but it was ordered otherwise. The little we know of his last days is from the simple narrative of a native woman, who was bringing the Dürings' little girl to England in the same ship. Sara Bickersteth was, as Johnson himself described her, " the first of her nation who had tasted that the Lord is gracious," and to her was granted the sacred privilege of tending her beloved pastor in his dying hour. It appears that within three days of his embarkation the symptoms of fever appeared, and day by day it grew worse and worse. On Saturday, 3rd May, he said to his weeping attendant, " I think I cannot live ; " and then delirium set in; but amidst his wanderings he spoke of his faithful African helpers, and called for his brother missionary, Düring, " to tell him all he had to say." Then reason returned, and he spoke lovingly of his poor wife, and of his longing wish to see her before he died; and then he tried to comfort his poor weeping convert, and gave her full directions as to what she was to do when she got to England.

It was a touching scene—the dying missionary in the cabin of the ship; the black girl—his own child in the faith, watching by his berth; the white baby in her arms, quite unconscious of what it all meant. Johnson asked her to read the twenty-third Psalm; "And when I had read it," proceeds her touching narrative, "he said to me, 'I am going to die; pray for me;' and I prayed the Lord Jesus to take him the right way." Then he sent a charge to the Society to send a good minister to Regent's-Town, and added, "If I am not able to go back, you must tell David Noah to do his duty; for if Noah say, 'Because massa dead, I can do nothing,' he must pray, and God will help him, and so we shall meet in heaven." The last words that Sara Bicker-steth could catch were these—"I cannot live. God calls me; I shall go to Him this night."

So died William Augustine Bernard Johnson, on the 4th May, 1823, at the early age of thirty-five.   Like Judson, he lies in his ocean grave until the sea shall give up her dead.   Like him, he needs no other monument than the blessed work which he was permitted to accomplish, and which has since grown into such vast proportions that Sierra Leone has ceased to be a missionary station, and has become a fully organized native Church.   When its first bishop, Dr. Vidal, reached the colony in 1853, three thousand candidates renewed their baptismal vows at his confirmation.   The colony is now marked out into its several parishes, rejoices in its native pastorate, has its college affiliated to an English university, and has sent out, under the first black bishop of modern times, its own missions along the course of the Niger, and into that vast interior which it was the burning desire of Johnson to see evangelized.

He was pre-eminently a missionary of God's making and of God's sending. As we trace his history, from the days of his poverty and despair at Whitechapel, until he stood forth as the ambassador of life and consolation to the crushed and bleeding sons of Africa, we feel that he had been prepared for his special work by the power of grace, and the discipline of suffering. And as we contrast the state of Sierra Leone, when Johnson first knew it, with what it was when he left it, and still more with what it has become in our own day, we bless the mercy and the love which raised up men like him to consummate the efforts which had been already set on foot, for the emancipation of the slave.

The following passage from the pen of his biographer may form a suitable close to this brief sketch of his memorable life:—

"Isolate, for a moment, the case of Regent's Town, and let it be regarded with close attention. Here is a single man, but just escaped from a London workshop, employed in organizing, civilizing, and humanizing a large body of rescued slaves, of a different race, and of various other tongues. In a wonderfully short space of time he so gains the affections of these poor savages that a large Christian village arises, almost as if by magic. Streets and gardens, a church and schools, fields and farm-yards, are occupied and cultivated by hundreds of willing hearts and hands. *At once*, without any delay, a congregation of redeemed and saved men and women is seen. The church is filled to overflowing; the schools are crowded with eager learners; hundreds press forward to beg for the benefit of the Christian Sacraments. Meanwhile, industry and its fruits abound on every side; and purity of morals, such as no English village knows, universally prevails. Such are the results of even three or four years' labour; may we not reasonably ask,—when did the religion of Rome, or of the East, or when did the philanthropy of rationalistic philosophers, produce such a wondrous transformation as this?"

VIII.

JOHN HUNT. FIJI, 1838—1848.

FIJI has been lately annexed to the British Crown, and our leading newspapers contain frequent advertisements setting forth, in attractive colours, the great advantages which may be enjoyed by emigrants to this new and thriving colony. Amongst others are named the peaceful and industrious habits of the great body of the native population, and the steady progress which they are making in the arts and pursuits of civilized life.

It will be worth our while to contrast all this with the state of Fiji fifty years ago. We shall then be in a better position to estimate the marvellous and salutary influence which missionary enterprise has exercised upon it, and to form some idea of its deep obligations to the man who was the chief instrument in bringing that influence to bear.

The Fiji group consists of some hundred islands, lying at seven days' distance from New Zealand; of these, the two principal, known respectively as Viti Levu and Vanua Levu, contain one hundred and fifty thousand inhabitants, and are each about the size of Devonshire. The population of all the other islands, when taken together, amounts to about a similar number. On these islands, Nature seems to have lavished her richest treasures of fruitfulness and beauty. "The tree, the shrub, the flower, the leaf, are all fresh and strong, and brought to perfection. New and beautiful varieties meet the eye at every turn. Fruits and flowers teem by the roadside; the fruit is good for food, and the colours of the flowers defy description."

But when men turned to contemplate the moral aspect of the scene, it was hideous in the extreme. To speak of the treachery and ferocity of the inhabitants were to say but little. The rage of civilized man was only like the restless tossings of a baby, when compared with the passion of a Fijian savage. Let those who have witnessed it describe it : " The forehead is filled with wrinkles ; the large nostrils distend and fairly smoke ; the staring eyeballs grow red and gleam with terrible flashings ; the mouth is distended into a murderous and disdainful grin ; the whole body quivers with excitement ; every muscle is strained, and the clenched fist seems eager to bathe itself in the blood of him who has roused this demon of fury."

Infanticide and cannibalism flourished in even darker forms than in other savage lands. Two-thirds of all the infants were killed at birth, and every village had an executioner appointed to carry out this deed of blood. Those who survived were early trained to the darkest deeds. Dead bodies were handed over to young children to hack and hew ; living captives were given up to them to mutilate and torture. No marvel if we read that sick and aged parents were put out of the way by the clubs of their own offspring, and that hoary hairs and failing strength excited neither reverence nor compassion. As to cannibalism, it had become an Epicurean art. The mother rubbed a reeking portion of the horrible repast on the lips of her own infant, to generate an early taste for human blood. It was no uncommon thing for a man to select his best wife or his most tender child for the dreadful festival, and even to invite his friends to the awful banquet. Ra Undreundu kept a registry, by means of stones, of the bodies which he had eaten, and they numbered 900! The only word in the Fijian language for the human body when deprived of life was "Vakalu," and that word included in it the idea of cannibalism! The horrid practice mingled itself with all the acts of life and worship. The building of a canoe, the burial of the dead, the payment of a tax, and even the taking down of a mast, were each accompanied by this revolting ceremonial. A chief has been known to kill eight or ten men in order to make rollers for the launching of his canoe, and the ovens were previously ablaze to cook them for his banquet. We must draw the veil over still darker scenes, which will not endure recital in Christian ears.

It was to such a people that John Hunt was destined to be a missionary and (we use the word with reverence) a saviour. Agents of the Wesleyan Missionary Society had reached their shores from the Friendly Islands in 1834, and the accounts transmitted by them to England led to the issue of a remarkable appeal entitled, "Pity poor Fiji!" This document not only pointed out the miserable condition of these wretched heathens, but gave hope, from the success which had already accompanied the first missionary efforts amongst them, that the Gospel would yet win its way in these benighted islands.

Hunt was at this time a student in the Wesleyan Academy at Hoxton, and had his heart set on going out to Africa; but a man was sorely wanted for Fiji, and the lot fell most unexpectedly upon him. His previous history was a remarkable one. He had been brought up as a farm-boy, but he was neither handy nor expert at common work, and was often laughed at as a simpleton by his fellow-labourers. But for all that, the Lincoln-shire plough-boy meditated great things. He had often heard his father, who had served as a sailor under Nelson, tell stirring stories of bravery and adventure, and in his secret soul he resolved to be a hero. His heroism, however, was to be exhibited on a very different field from any which he had been contemplating. His earliest religious impressions appear to have been connected with a deep anxiety felt by him for the salva-tion of his own mother, and these were soon deepened by recovery from a brain-fever, and by the instructions of Methodist preachers in the district where he lived.

The Genius of Poetry found Burns at the plough, and the Genius of Missionary Enter-prise found Hunt at a like employment. At nineteen years of age he was fortunate enough to be hired by a farmer who was a reading man. Hitherto Hunt had seen no books except the Bible and the Pilgrim's Progress; but now he began to read such works as

Paley's Evidences, and Dwight's Theology, and Horne's Introduction, and he gave up all his spare time to mental improvement. Mason on Self-knowledge was the book, however, that took most thorough hold of him, and did most for the formation of his character. Very few would have suspected that under his blue smock there throbbed a heart that was beginning to feel the consciousness of a power, the existence of which it scarcely dared to credit. But the time to test it was at hand. In the unavoidable absence of a local preacher, he was asked to address a little congregation in the humble chapel. With trembling and reluctance he consented, but he did his part so ably and so well that he was asked to repeat the effort elsewhere. A Methodist preacher, who happened to hear him, had the sagacity to perceive from his rough but vigorous speech, and in his apt and ready power of illustration, that John Hunt was no common man.

He sounded him on the subject of his becoming a preacher, and the honest ploughman, while shrinking, under the deep sense of his own unworthiness, from such an office, confessed an "ambition to go to the Cape, as a servant to Laidman Hodgson," a missionary whom he had often heard preach on the circuit, and whom he thought he would be able "to assist a little, not only in gardening, but in Sunday-school teaching, and other humble ministrations." The letter of the preacher, recommending him to the Missionary Committee, amused the secretaries, and seemed to them a piece of good-natured extravagance ; but when they came to have an interview with the young man, they found that he was far beyond the average standard, and he was at once admitted to the Institution at Hoxton. His progress in study soon justified their choice, and at the end of his second year he was sent to the Oxford circuit, where his earnest, thoughtful, and manly speech commanded attention and respect. There was a flame of genius in his eye when he warmed to his subject, and a token of might in the stretching out of his long and sinewy arm, as in bold but loving accents he addressed his fellow-men. Africa was upper-most in his thoughts, and his daily prayer was for " fitness for the work of God in that dark continent." But he was destined for another field, and his nomination to it came to him both as a surprise and a disappoint-ment. He was summoned to the Mission House in 1838, and asked whether he would go to Fiji. The question startled him, and he asked time to consider it. Returning to Hoxton, he burst into the room of a fellow-student, and in quick, excited tones told him of the unexpected proposal. His friend, thinking only of the hardships and peril of such a mission, began to sympathize with him. But he had not read the secret of Hunt's deep emotion. " Oh, that's not it," exclaimed the impassioned youth; " I'll tell you what it is : that poor girl in Lincolnshire will never go with me to Fiji; her mother will never consent to it." The truth was, that that strong noble heart of his had been linked in love, for the last six years, to Hannah Summers, and he, whom neither cannibalism nor paganism could affright, felt dismayed at the possibility of being parted from her for ever. At his friend's suggestion he sat down instantly and wrote her a loving and straightforward letter, every line of which made it plain that, if he had doubts about others, he had none about her. Still his heart was distressed, and he moved in and out amongst his fellow-students with an anxious and dejected air. But as quickly as posts could travel in those days, came back the reply of that noble girl, and Hunt burst once more into his friend's chamber, and with beaming face and cheery voice exclaimed, "It's all right! She'll go with me anywhere!"

About one o'clock on the 14th February, 1838, the formal decision of the Missionary Committee was given; at half-past two Hunt was on the coach, and next morning he was at home. On the 6th of March he was married, and on the 29th of April he and his devoted wife sailed for Sydney. There he met John Williams, the future martyr of Erromanga, and it is remarkable that they left Sydney upon the same day for their respective mission fields.

Upon landing at Fiji on the 22nd of December, the young missionary and his wife found that they must go to Rewa, a solitary and distant station on Viti Levu, and take up their lonely residence amongst a savage people, of whose language they were in utter ignorance. But undismayed they went to their arduous post, and instantly Hunt began his study of the language. They soon found that, so far as the butcheries and cruelties of the people were concerned, "the half had not been told them." The king, however, was favourable, and one or two of the chiefs were ready to "*lotu*," that is, to profess the new religion; but their motives were of a very mixed nature, as may be gathered from the reply of one of them when asked whether he believed that Christianity was true; "True? Everything that comes from white man's country is true; muskets and gun-powder are true; your religion must be true!" Still, their adherence prepared the way for the Gospel, and the people were more willing to listen to it when the chiefs had once set the example. It was not long before the

power of truth began to tell, and real conversions followed; but as soon as they took
place persecution began. The priests and
heathen chiefs plundered every one who had
been guilty of the *lotu*. Strange to say, it
was the influence of the king, himself a
heathen, that stayed the rising hostility.
His own brother, who had been a leader in
the pillage of the Christians, was severely
reproved by him; and when, notwithstanding
this, he threatened the missionaries in the
king's presence, the king significantly said,
"If you injure the missionaries, I will begin
to eat chiefs." Every one knew the meaning
of that threat; the offender begged forgiveness, and the persecution ceased.

At the end of seven months it was thought
desirable that Hunt should leave Rewa, and
settle at Somosomo, a town of great importance on another island. Tuithakau, the
king, and his two sons, were persons of great
influence, and having heard of the missions at
Lakemba, they had put in a plea for teachers
for themselves. The Somosomo people were
more than ordinarily savage, and were re-

garded with as much horror by the other Fijians as the Fijians themselves were regarded by the English. No missionary had ever visited Somosomo; no native of the place had ever *lotued.* Only one white man had ventured there, and he had been barbarously murdered a short time before; but thither the heroic missionary and his wife repaired, together with another devoted couple, Mr. and Mrs. Lythe, and here the next three years of their consecrated lives were spent.

Notwithstanding the king's invitation, their reception was cold and cheerless, and the sights and scenes amidst which they had to live were appalling in the extreme. Within a week news came that the king's youngest son was lost at sea. Forthwith an order was issued that sixteen women, some of them of high rank, should be strangled, and despite of Hunt's entreaties they were put to death, and then burned in front of the mission-house, amidst the blast of conchs and the yells of incarnate demons. Some months later, eleven men were dragged with ropes to the ovens, and roasted for a banquet; and when the missionary's wife closed the window-blinds against the sight and stench of the horrid festival, the infuriated natives threatened to burn down the house unless they were re-opened!

Sickness and domestic bereavements came and added to their sorrows, and yet we read in Hunt's journal at this period that " trials and privations are words seldom used by us, and are things that are thought much more of by our dear friends at home than by ourselves." Take one scene from this period of his life. It is a Sunday evening, and their place of worship is a gloomy room, under a low thatched roof, with a small chamber at one end, partitioned off with mats. In this room stands the preacher, with a visible congregation of two men, and an invisible audience of two women. The two men are his brother missionary and a young Englishman, whose life he has lately saved from the club of a murderous chief. The two unseen listeners are the missionaries' wives, each with a new-born baby, one of them being the preacher's firstborn child, and it is dying. But the text is from the first chapter of St. James : " My brethren, count it all joy when ye fall into divers temptations; knowing this, that the trial of your faith worketh patience."

Three days after this the child was dead; and as the mother bent over her lifeless babe, she had to encounter, when she looked up, dark savage faces mocking at her grief. Oh! could she only lay her little one in a quiet grave in some Christian land, the trial would not be so severe; but yet that little grave "consecrated Fiji as the missionaries' burial-ground, and the soil has become very wealthy since."

The king of Somosomo, though he did not formally withdraw his protection from Hunt and his companions, forbad his people becoming Christians under pain of death. The missionaries could have withdrawn, had they so desired; and when Captain Wilkes, of the American Navy, visited the island in 1840, he was so pained with the sight of all their sufferings, that he offered to convey them to any other island; but they declined the offer, and persevered in their work. At length it was resolved that Mr. Hunt should leave, in order to occupy another station, which had been deprived of its missionary's services. The results of his three years' work in Somosomo had been only indirect, but they were far from being unimportant. Mr. Hunt, when leaving, could appeal to the following instances :—a town had been taken in war without a man being killed; a large canoe has been launched, and has made her first voyage without a single instance of cannibalism ; and the Somosomo people have feasted their superiors, the Mbau people, for several weeks without a single dead body. In the first instance we were *one cause*, instrumentally, of the people being spared ; in the second, perhaps the *only cause ;* and in the third, perhaps the only cause too; *but we had not directly to interfere;* for the influence which truth had on the minds of the people made our interference unnecessary.

Viwa, where the last six years of Hunt's life were spent, and where his greatest triumphs were won, was an important political centre, within a few miles of Mbau, the highest seat of Fiji power; the local chief was favourable, and some converts had been already made; but King Thakombau, "the butcher of his people," was fierce in his opposition, and the bloody wars in which he was constantly engaged made the missionary's position exceedingly perilous. Still with undaunted bravery and heroic patience he went on. Now he is at work upon his translation, and to him belongs the honour of giving the New Testament to Fiji in its native tongue; now he is travelling his eleven hundred miles in a single twelvemonth, and making known everywhere the story of peace; now he is organizing schools, and training the most promising of his converts as native teachers.

Amidst troubles and perils, amidst wars and rumours of wars, we find Hunt (to use his own favourite expression) "turning care into prayer," and steadily pursuing the one purpose of his life. "I must be on the full stretch," was his constant apology when friends thought he worked too hard. What that apology implied will be best understood by a glance at his labours. There was first of all the difficult task of conquering the language; then the ceaseless endeavour to restrain the cruel dispositions of the chiefs; then the incessant effort to instil some ideas of God and goodness into dark and savage minds. One day he is writing upon his favourite subject of sanctification, and preparing his manuscript for the press; another day he is reading Swift or Byron, and cultivating his mental powers by the study of English literature and the Greek Testament; always he is taking the bright view of things; and if there be a single spot of sunshine in the landscape, he is sure to find it out. And he tries to spread sunshine, as well as to enjoy it; acting as nurse and doctor to the sick and dying, carrying little comforts from the mission house to Fijian hovels, and instructing the wretched natives in a thousand little arts of decency and civilization, whilst he is ever trying to lead them to still higher things.

A great movement at length took place

amongst the people. The priests had predicted a terrible drought in consequence of the *lotu*, but it did not come. The faith of the people in paganism began to be shaken. The queen of Viwa became a Christian. Thakombau's personal friend and generalissimo, the redoubtable Verani, who has been styled " the Napoleon of Fiji," followed her example, and was baptized by the name of Elijah.. The great canoe, which he used to launch for war and bloodshed, was now constantly employed in carrying the messenger of mercy to. the distant islands. Verani himself became a preacher. Thakombau endeavoured to dissuade him, and the people expected that he would take summary vengeance on the apostate; but to their astonishment he exclaimed, "Did I not tell you that we could not turn Verani? He is a man of one heart: when he was with us, he was fully one with us; now that he is a Christian, he is decided, and not to be moved." This kingliness of consistency began to tell on others, and ere long the converts were reckoned by thousands.

Hunt was a "Wesleyan of the Wesleyans;" and the movement, as it sped, bore marks of the system out of which it grew; but it was no marvel that fierce cannibals, by whatever agency they were brought to repentance, should exhibit those agonies of sorrow, and those excitements of conviction, which were manifested amongst the Fijians. For days and nights together they gave way to the wildest grief, they fainted away from sheer exhaustion, then prayed themselves into an agony again, and then passed into a state of utter insensibility. There was, however, a real and abiding work beneath all this, and Hunt knew how to distinguish it. "There are here," he says, "two conversions, one from heathenism to Christianity as a system, and a second from sin to God. Both these are of the greatest importance: without the first there is no hope of the second. We seldom witness anything like penitence in a heathen. Generally it is not until they have professed Christianity for some time that they sincerely seek the Lord."

The claims upon his thought and labour

during this exciting period, and still more
during the reaction which followed, and then
the responsibility and care which came upon
him with all the exigencies and demands of
a settled Christian population, began to tell
upon his stalwart frame.   The pale face, and
feverish pulse, and failing appetite told that
something severe had been going on behind
the outer scene.   There was something
solemn—almost a mystery of heavenliness—
about that tall, thin, stooping figure, as with
earnest eyes and feeble steps he still endeavoured to carry on his work.   What a
contrast to the man of iron strength who
had come up to London from the fields of
Lincolnshire some twelve years before!   It
was soon evident that he was dying, and the
native Christians met and entreated God to
spare him to them.   Elijah Verani's prayer
was touching: "O Lord, we know that we
are very evil! but spare Thy servant: if
one must die, take *me! take ten of us!*   But
spare Thy servant to preach Christ to the
people!"

It was not to be.   The last conflict was at

hand. Hunt died with his armour on, and entered heaven with the note of triumph on his lips—" Hallelujah." His coffin needed no earthly heraldry to emblazon it. It bore the simple inscription :—

JOHN HUNT

SLEPT IN JESUS OCTOBER 4TH, 1848.

AGED 36 YEARS.

Thakombau came to look upon the dead face of the teacher before whom he had often quailed, and to do honour to the man whom in his inmost heart he could not but revere. Hunt had left a message of love and prayer for the royal savage, who as he listened to it was deeply moved. The missionary did not live to see his prayer answered, but others did; and when, some years later, Thakombau was publicly baptized, the congregation which witnessed his Christian profession was a strange one ;—husbands whose wives he had dishonoured; widows whose husbands he had slain; sisters whose brothers he had strangled; relatives whose friends he had eaten ; children who formerly had vowed to avenge in his blood the wrongs inflicted on their parents.

Hunt's work was an abiding one. The late Dr. Harvey, Professor of Botany in the University of Dublin, visited Fiji in 1850, two years after Hunt's death, and has left the following testimony: "I speak from personal observation, having visited the Wesleyan Missions at the Friendly and Fiji Islands. I know something, therefore, of the work that is actually going forward in the Pacific; and as I am in no way connected with this mission, and, from my predilections as a Churchman, not over-disposed to sympathize with a body of Dissenters, you may, I hope, regard me as an unprejudiced witness, if I speak favourably of what I have seen. . . . It has pleased God remarkably to bless the labours of His servants, who had so long watered the ground, not only with their tears, but with their blood. Some await in Fijian graves a glorious resurrection; but others who have for long time ' gone forth weeping, bearing precious seed,' are now returning joyful, ' bringing their sheaves with them.'

Heathenism is everywhere on the decline. Neither heathen temple nor heathen priest any longer remains at Bau. In that late abode of butchery and lust, the Christian congregation meeting every Lord's-day numbers over a thousand. Some 70,000 throughout the various islands are at least nominally Christian, and thousands more are willing to come under mission teaching, if only missionaries and native teachers can be sent to them. And if nothing interfere to blight present prospects, please God, a few more years will witness the demoniacs of Fiji no longer ' naked, and cutting themselves with stones,' but redeemed to Christ, ' sitting, clothed, and in their right minds.' "

These hopeful anticipations have been to a great extent realized. Fiji is not only a gem in the British crown, but a precious jewel in the missionary diadem; and to John Hunt, above all other men, belongs the honour of having placed it there!

IX.

CAPTAIN ALLEN GARDINER, R.N.
ZULULAND AND SOUTH AMERICA, 1835—1851.

THE tragical fate which befell this heroic man, in his noble endeavour to introduce Christianity into Terra del Fuego, has made his name to be a household word, and has won for him a distinguished place in the history of missionary adventure. But it is not generally known that Allen Gardiner had been a missionary pioneer during sixteen years of his previous life, and had already endured hardships and privations of no ordinary kind in his efforts to prepare the way for the Gospel, both in South Africa and in South America. He was a layman, and, though urged to enter into holy orders, pre-ferred to continue one to the end, because he believed that in that capacity he could best promote God's glory, and clear the track for the ordained messengers of peace. His plans were not always the wisest or the best constructed, but his spirit and resolution were of the loftiest type, and in all our missionary annals there is no one who can more justly claim as his own the apostolic motto, " In journeyings often."

Born in 1794, the son of a Berkshire squire, he showed an early predilection for a sailor's life. While he was still a child he exercised his ingenuity in sketching a plan for cutting the French fleet out of Rochelle harbour. A love of adventure was early manifested by his writing out a vocabulary of African words from " Mungo Park's Travels," and by his sleeping all night upon the floor, in the hope, as he said, that he would thereby inure himself to hardship, as he " intended to travel all over the world."

At sixteen he entered the navy, and having distinguished himself as a midshipman in an engagement between the *Phœbe* and the *Essex*, he was sent home as lieutenant in charge of the prize. Four years after this (1820) we find him at Penang, in the *Daunt-*

less, and it was here that the early but neglected instructions of a pious and departed mother began to tell. His father had drawn up a touching record of her last days, but had not shown it to his son. It happened, however, that a Christian lady, who was present at her death, lent the narrative to the young sailor before he sailed from Portsmouth, and allowed him to copy it. Gardiner had wandered far from her early teaching; but this memoir recalled him. He bought a Bible, but was so much ashamed to be seen doing so, that he watched the bookseller's shop until he saw there were no customers inside, and then he ventured in and made the purchase. That Bible and that narrative accompanied him to Penang. While there a wise and kindly letter received from his mother's friend set him upon examining the one and reflecting upon the other, and the result was that the dashing young naval officer gave his heart to God.

His duties led him at this time to the coasts of South America, and he began to take that deep interest in the aborigines which never afterwards forsook him, and in the exercise of which he laid down his life. He had witnessed the blessed results of missionary effort in Tahiti, and when he came back to England on sick leave, he pleaded the cause of the poor Indians with the London Missionary Society, and placed his services at their disposal. The Society did not see its way to undertake the mission, and Allen Gardiner resumed his naval duties, and became a married man. His wife was delicate, and her increasing illness led them eventually to reside in the Isle of Wight. At length she was taken from him, and beside her bier he made a solemn vow to dedicate himself more especially to the service of God. His tastes and training pointed out to him the path of a missionary explorer, and he determined to become a pioneer in some of those dark regions of the earth which had not yet been visited by the light of the Gospel.

His steps were directed in the first instance to Southern Africa. Our colonists had been pushing their way amongst the warlike

Kaffirs, and frequent conflicts had taken place between them, but no one as yet had dreamt of subduing them to Christ. The honour of starting the first missionary settlement in Zululand belongs to Captain Gardiner. This is an interesting fact, when taken in connection with all that has since rendered that country so familiar to Englishmen, both in a political and a religious point of view. He induced a Pole named Berken to accompany him, and the history of their perils and adventures reads like a strange romance. Now with their own hands they are digging their horses out of the morasses into which they have sunk; now they are swimming the swollen rivers, at the peril of their lives, and lying down upon the banks, wet and hungry, to be awakened from their uncomfortable repose by the snorting of hippopotami, as the huge animals come trampling through the crushed and quivering reeds. At length Gardiner reached the rude capital of Dingairn, an able but ferocious chief, who was the terror of all white settlers, and the tyrant of his own people.

Over this man he contrived to gain a marvellous influence, even inducing him, though he steadily refused to become a Christian, to grant ground for a missionary settlement.

Gardiner now took up his residence at Port Natal, his only possessions being "his clothes, his saddle, a spoon, and a New Testament." The colony, if such it could be called, consisted of a few miserable hovels, in which some thirty rough Englishmen resided, surrounded by a multitude of fugitive Zulus, who acted as their servants. Our pioneer made himself at home amongst this motley company, and did what he could to instruct them. It was no new thing to him, as a naval officer, to read the Church of England service on Sunday mornings; so he gathered the white men under the shadow of a stately tree, and read to them words which they had almost forgotten, but which came back to them like the tones of their mother's voice. In the afternoon he collected the Kaffirs, and, with the help of an interpreter, explained to them the simplest facts of Bible history. Nor were his week-days unemployed. He opened a school for the wretched native children, dressed them in the first clothing they had ever known, and became himself their patient schoolmaster. Nor was this all. He aided the colonists with his advice and succour in founding their first regular town, and on the 25th June, 1835, it sprang into existence as " Durban."

Troubles arose between the colonists and Dingairn. The Zulus who worked for the English had fled from his tyranny, and he threatened to come down upon the settlement with fire and foray. Gardiner appeared in the new character of an ambassador, and presented himself at the kraal of the royal savage in his full uniform. This made a deep impression; but the known and approved character of the ambassador made a deeper one; and the result of this strange interview was that Dingairn constituted our hero his plenipotentiary, and made him governor of " all the country of the white people's fold," that is, in other words, of the territory which we now call Natal. This induced Gardiner to revisit England in order to consult the Government on the political situation, and the Church Missionary Society concerning the religious one. He soon returned with a missionary staff, and was warmly received by Dingairn, who however was apprised that the missionaries could not hold secular appointments, and that these should be given to officers of the British Crown.

For a time all went on prosperously; but complications, for which the missionaries were in no way responsible, soon arose between the whites and the Zulus. Covetousness and greed on the one side induced revenge and treachery on the other. War and rapine followed; the missionary settlement had to be abandoned; and Gardiner, after more than three years of earnest labour in Natal, left Africa with a heavy heart, and sought a new field for his exertions.

His thoughts naturally reverted to the Indians of South America, and more especially to those of the Pampas and of Chili, who in past years had not only stirred his compassion by their spiritual destitution, but had also excited his admiration by the heroic stand which they had made for their independence. He reached Rio Janeiro in July 1838, and immediately began a series of indefatigable journeyings and investigations. We can give but a passing glance at them. He travelled to Monte Video and Buenos Ayres, and thence to Mendoza. In fourteen days he crossed nine hundred miles of the Pampas, then scaled the heights of the Cordilleras, and after eleven days of incessant toil reached Santiago, on the Chilian side of the Andes. From Santiago he travelled to Concepcion, thence to New Guinea, and from that he made his way to Valparaiso. During these journeys he had frequent interviews with native chiefs, but the results were not satisfactory; "They did not want a missionary." Many of them had suffered so fearfully at the hands of white men, and especially of Spaniards, that they looked upon all strangers with suspicion. Some of them were even then under going the miseries of an exterminating warfare from the races which called themselves civilized, and there was no opening for the introduction of the gospel of peace. In other districts, where these difficulties did not exist, the jealousy of the authorities and the opposition of the Romish priesthood precluded all hope of doing good; and so, after two years of fruitless effort, he quitted South America, and directed his steps to New Guinea, where he was met by the sullen suspicions of the Dutch, who could not bring themselves to believe that an English officer was free from political designs, and who only looked upon his missionary pronouncements as a cloak for these.

Baffled successively upon two continents, and now once again in the Malay Archipelago, he conceived the plan with which his last and best known enterprise was to be associated. In a letter written at this time to a friend he says: "Having at last abandoned all hope of reaching the Indian inhabitants where they are most civilized and least migratory, my thoughts are necessarily turned toward the South. Happily for us, and I trust eventually for the poor Indians, the Falkland Islands are now under the British flag; and although the settlement is poor, still it is the resort of numbers of whalers, and of the small sealing vessels which frequent the Straits of Magellan. The Patagonians about Gregory Bay, in the north-eastern part of the strait, have always evinced a friendly disposition to foreigners, and it is to that spot I am now particularly turning my attention. We purpose to proceed to Berkeley Sound in the Falkland Islands. Making this our place of residence, I intend to cross over in a sealer, and to spend the summer among the Patagonians. Who can tell but the Falkland Islands, so admirably suited for the purpose, may become the key to the aborigines, both of Patagonia and Terra del Fuego?"

He went to the Cape of Good Hope, and fetched his family with him from thence to the Falklands. Leaving them there in a lonely wooden hut, on that treeless, shrubless shore, he set off with his servant in a crazy schooner for the stormy Straits of Magellan. Here he came into contact with the Fuegian dwellers on the islands, and found them to be barbarians of the lowest type, whom neither gifts nor kindliness could conciliate, and who were evidently determined to give no countenance to their white visitors. He therefore resolved on making his way to a tribe of Patagonians on the mainland, concerning whom he had received some information, and with whom a Spanish Creole had been living for some twelve years. This wild adventurer had gained considerable influence amongst them, and proved most useful to Gardiner as an interpreter. A chieftain named Wissale was particularly friendly, and promised a welcome to the captain, if he would come back and set up a mission amongst his people; so Gardiner returned full of hope and thankfulness to his sorry home upon the Falklands, determined to bring back his family with him, and to settle amongst the Patagonians.

But he was fated to be disappointed. The whalers would not undertake the perilous voyage for £300, which was all that he had to offer them. His applications to the Church Missionary Society were not successful, for at that time they had not the means to undertake a new mission. So he resolved on returning to England, and pleading in person the cause of Patagonia amongst British Christians. Even in this his hopes were frustrated. His appeal was met with apathy and coldness; but nothing could chill the warmth of his burning missionary zeal. Failing in his main object, he endeavoured to further it indirectly by obtaining a grant of Bibles and Testaments, and set sail for Rio Janeiro in order to distribute them. This was in 1843; and his perils and experiences, as he travelled from port to port, and from place to place, would supply a chapter of strange adventure. One thing resulted from it, for which he was thankful, and that was a promise of £100 a year from English congregations in South America towards the establishment of a Patagonian mission.

Strengthened by this encouragement, he returned again to his native land, where his eloquent and earnest appeals were more successful than those of his previous visit. The foundations of a missionary society for Patagonia and Terra del Fuego were laid in 1844, and before the year expired he was again upon his old ground, along with a Mr. Hunt, who resigned an endowed school in Kendal in order to accompany him, and to prepare the way for an ordained clergyman. Once more the story of fatigue and danger was enacted in reaching the natives; but somehow things were changed since Gardiner had left. Wissale proved hostile, and attempted Gardiner's life; a Spanish padre had arrived, and had preoccupied the ground; and the brave pioneer, disappointed but not dismayed, took advantage of the arrival of a British ship to return home and wait a more auspicious opportunity. Some will say that he exhibited less patience than courage, and that as he was prone to be rapid and resolute in making his beginnings, so was he also prone to relinquish his projects without sufficient cause. But the whole life of the man contradicts this theory. His own view of the case is the true explanation of his conduct, and it is summed up in the following passage of his journal : " We can never do wrong in casting the Gospel net on any side or in any place. During many a dark and wearisome night we may appear to have toiled in vain, but it will not be always so." "If they persecute you in one city, flee ye to another."

It was no marvel if, after such failures, his supporters in England began to hesitate about further attempts; but his own resolution remained unshaken. "Whatever course you may determine upon," said our hero, "I have made up my mind to go back again to South America, and leave no stone un- turned, no effort untried, to establish a mission amongst the aboriginal tribes. They have a right to be instructed in the Gospel of Christ. While God gives me strength, failure shall not daunt me. This, then, is my firm resolve—to go back and make further researches among the natives of the interior, whether any possible opening may be found which has hitherto escaped me through the Spanish Americans, or whether Terra del Fuego is the only ground left us for our last attempt.   This I intend to do at my own risk, whether the Society is broken up or not.   Fund the money which belongs to the Society, and wait to see the result of the researches now to be made.   Our Saviour has given a commandment to preach the Gospel even to the ends of the earth.   He will provide for the fulfilment of His own purpose.   Let us only obey!"

The deeds of the man were as heroic as his words.   In 1846, we find him in company with a Spanish Protestant, making his way through Bolivia, despite of fever and opposition, to reach the Indians who lay beyond; and presently we discover him once again travelling up and down through England, reporting the openings he had discovered, and endeavouring to fire his auditors with something of his own burning enthusiasm. If he had found it difficult to urge his committee on, they now found that it was impossible to hold him back.   Their means were not sufficient to fit out such an expedition as he wished for, but he induced them to consent to an experimental one on a smaller scale. With four sailors and one ship-carpenter, a dingey, a whaleboat, and two wigwams, he started in 1848 in the barque *Clymene*, bound for Payta. He landed at Picton Island, where the thievish propensities of the Fuegians soon made it manifest that a mission amongst them could only be safely conducted afloat, that for this purpose a ship would be required, and that the boats which he had brought from England were unsuited for his hazardous enterprise in such stormy latitudes. And so the dauntless sailor returned to England to urge the need of larger means and a more thorough equipment.

He found it impossible to stir up the generosity of British Christians to the liberality that was required. No one knew better than he did what was absolutely needed for such a project, and again and again he pressed his convictions concerning it upon the Society at home. But their funds were small, and it may be mentioned that of the £1000 collected he gave £300 himself. So,

sooner than abandon his enterprise, he re-
luctantly resolved to modify his plans, and
reduce them to the lowest estimate, in the
self-denying but delusive hope that some
additional danger and hardship, endured by
himself and his companions, would compen-
sate for the absence of those better equip-
ments which his nautical experience had so
wisely suggested at the first.

On the 7th September, 1850, the expedition sailed. The names of the deathless
seven deserve to be recorded. Allen Gardiner was the chief, and was accompanied by
two catechists—Surgeon Williams and John
Maidment; three Cornish fishermen—Pearce,
Badcock, and Bryant, well accustomed to
stormy seas in the Irish Channel; and a
ship-carpenter named Joseph Erwin, who
had been with Gardiner on his previous
voyage, and now volunteered for this fresh
service, declaring that to be with such a
captain "was like a heaven upon earth, he
was such a man of prayer." They were all
men of simple piety, and went to the work
with holy resolution. From first to last

not a jarring word was heard in that devoted company, and their one object was "to serve the good Master in whose name they had gone forth." The *Ocean Queen*, bound for San Francisco, gave them a passage, and undertook to land them at Terra del Fuego, with their two launches—the *Pioneer* and the *Speedwell*, and provisions for six months.

And now we come to the story of the saddest disaster in the records of missionary enterprise. It had been arranged that provisions for another six months should follow the party, but the committee could not find any ship that would consent to go out of its course to Picton Island, and they had therefore to forward the supplies to the Falklands. The governor there arranged to send them on, but by a sad fatality the vessel was wrecked, and the master of a second disobeyed orders, and so the missionary party were left unprovided. Meantime they had landed, but were compelled by the plundering habits and hostile attitude of the natives to re-embark, and seek shelter in a distant and retired bay, where they settled down in two companies, and waited in longing expectation for the promised relief. The storms crippled their boats, and destroyed one of them. Their nets were torn to pieces by the action of the ice, and as by an unfortunate oversight their powder had been forgotten on board the *Ocean Queen*, they could obtain no fresh supplies of food. At length their stores were becoming exhausted, and they had to subsist mainly on limpets, mussels, and wild celery. Scurvy broke out amongst them, and added its horrors to those of hunger. One by one they died upon that desert shore, and Gardiner was the last survivor of the gallant band!

Twenty days after his death, the *John Davison*, under Captain Smyly, sailed from Monte Video to enquire after them, and soon anchored in Banner Cove. He found a direction painted on the rocks—" Gone to Spaniard Harbour." Let us tell the sequel in Captain Smyly's words :—

" Oct. 22, 1851. Ran to Spaniard Harbour. Blowing a severe gale. Went on shore, and found a boat with one person dead inside; another body we found on the beach, another buried. These, we have every reason to believe, are Pearce, Williams, and Badcock. The sight was awful in the extreme. The two captains who were with me in the boat cried like children. Books, papers, medicine were strewed along the beach, and on the boats, deck, and cuddy. ... But we had no time to make further search, as the gale came on so hard. It gave us barely time to bury the corpses on the beach and get on board. The gale continued to increase, so that it drove us from our anchorage and out to sea. ... I have never found in my life such Christian fortitude, such patience and bearing, as in the records of these unfortunate men; they have never murmured, and Mr. Williams writes in one of his papers, and in the time of greatest distress, ' I am happy beyond all expression.' "

Meantime, H.M.S. *Dido* had been ordered by the Admiralty to search for the missionary party. She arrived in January 1852;

and Captain Morshead, guided by the sentence on the rocks, made for Spaniard Harbour. The following is his melancholy record :—

"Our notice was first attracted by a boat lying upon the beach. It was blowing very fresh from the south, and the ship rode uneasily at her anchor. I instantly sent Lieut. Pigott and Mr. Roberts to reconnoitre and return immediately, as I was anxious to get the ship to sea again in safety for the night; they returned shortly, bringing some books and papers, and having discovered the bodies of Captain Gardiner and Mr. Maidment unburied. . . . On one of the papers was written legibly, ' If you will walk along the beach for a mile and a half, you will find us in the other boat, hauled up in the mouth of a river at the head of the harbour, on the south side. Delay not—we are starving.' At this sad intelligence it was impossible to leave that night, though the weather looked very threatening. . . . We landed early next morning, January 22nd, and visited the spot where Captain Gardiner

and his comrade were lying, and then went
to the head of the harbour.   We found there
the wreck of a boat, with part of her gear
and stores, and a quantity of clothing, with
the remains of two bodies, which I conclude
to be Mr. Williams (surgeon), and John
Pearce (Cornish fisherman), as the papers
clearly show the death and burial of all the
rest of the mission party.   The two boats
were thus about a mile and a half apart.
Near the one where Captain Gardiner was
lying was a large cavern, called by him *Pioneer
Cavern*, where they kept their stores and
occasionally slept, and in that cavern Mr.
Maidment's body was found. . . .   Captain
Gardiner's body was lying beside the boat,
which apparently he had left, and being too
weak to climb into it again, had died by the
side of it.   We were directed to the cavern
by a hand painted on the rocks, with
Psalm lxii. 5-8 under it."

The words referred to are the following,
and the choice of them under such circumstances proves how strong and unshaken was
the faith of Gardiner and his companions :—

"*My soul, wait thou only upon God; for my
expectation is from Him.   He only is my rock
and my salvation; He is my defence; I shall
not be moved.   In God is my salvation and my
glory; the rock of my strength, and my refuge,
is in God.*"   The diaries, which fortunately
have been preserved, give a thrilling account
of those terrible months of patient endurance
and heroic resolution.   They tell moreover
of the love and consideration manifested by
the noble leader for his devoted band.   There
is something unspeakably touching in the
account of his getting Maidment to con-
struct crutches out of two forked sticks, so
that he might try to reach the other section
of his little company, and be a comfort to
them.   But his strength was not equal to
the effort, and he had to return to his boat.
There Maidment ministered to him, until he
too sank from exhaustion.   He had left a
little peppermint-water beside the bed of
his chief, and retired for rest to the cave,
but from it he never returned.

When we get our last glimpse of Gardiner,
he is weakly endeavouring, with his india-

rubber shoe, to scoop some water from a little pool which had trickled down at the stern of his boat. The last words he wrote were these: "Our dear brother left the boat on Tuesday at noon, and has not since returned; doubtless he is in the presence of his Redeemer, whom he served so faithfully. Yet a little while, and through grace we may join that blessed throng, to sing the praises of Christ through eternity. I neither hunger nor thirst, though five days without food! Marvellous lovingkindness to me a sinner!"

It was with sorrowing hearts the sailors of the *Dido* gathered together all that remained of this heroic band, and gave them Christian sepulture. The funeral service was appropriately read by a naval officer at the grave of Captain Gardiner and his comrades. The colours of the boats and ship were struck half-mast, and three volleys of musketry re-echoed on that lonely shore, as the last tribute of respect to a gallant and noble-minded Englishman.

No, we will not call it the last tribute of respect. In the letters and journals which he wrote in his "boat dormitory," he committed his mission to the care of the Christian Church, and sketched out the methods by which he thought it would be best advanced. That legacy of faith and love was administered to in the court of Christian charity by devoted men, who became his followers in the work on which he had set his heart. His own son was one of that heroic band. A mission-ship, called the *Allen Gardiner*, was built as the best memorial of his name. The Falklands have been since erected into an English bishopric, and the first occupant of the see is a man who had already devoted his life to God in the same missionary field where Captain Gardiner fell. Perhaps nothing short of the sad catastrophe which we have described would have awakened English Christians out of the apathy from which Gardiner had found it so impossible to arouse them, or kindled that zeal on behalf of South America which we are thankful to say has been evoked by his sad but glorious fate.

" The white foam crests the wave,
  The wind sweeps weirdly by ;
And whirling round with plaintive sound
  The stormy petrels cry.

" Amid the beetling rocks,
  In a chill cavern's shade,
Within the gloom of that strange dark tomb
  A dying bed is made !

" A gallant seaman there
  Casts round his sunken eyes :
Unblanched by fear, tho' grim Death is near,
  A noble Christian dies.

" No greed for yellow gold;
  To head no conquering band;
Not fame had led the sleeping dead
  To seek that savage land.

" I see a morning dawn,
  A King upon His throne,
And thousands stand at His right hand,
  Who well their work have done.

" With wreaths of victory crowned,
  Among that conquering band,
On the crystal sea his rest shall be,
  Who died for the Southern land ! "

X.

SOME sixty years ago a bright imaginative boy was lying, amongst the blaeberries, upon the bank of a stream that flowed close by his father's Highland cottage, as it nestled beneath the shadow of the Grampians. A short time before this he had fallen into the burn, and had narrowly escaped from drowning. The incident had made a deep impression upon him, which was further deepened by the reading of Buchanan's weird Gaelic poem, "The Day of Judgment," and Milton's sublime epic of "Paradise Lost," both of which exercised a strange fascination over his young mind. And so it came to pass that as he lay beside the stream he fell asleep, and dreamed a dream, which, whether we regard it as a prevision of his fancy, or as an intimation of his future destiny, may well be deemed remarkable. He saw above him a glorious light, from which there issued by-and-by a golden chariot studded with gems, and drawn by horses of fire. It reached his side, and he heard a voice saying to him, "Come up hither, I have work for thee to do." In the effort to arise the young sleeper awoke; but the remembrance of that dream never left him during a long life, and shortly before his death he related it to his grandson.

That youth was Alexander Duff, who was destined to be, in more senses than one, the first missionary of the Established Church of Scotland, and to exercise an influence upon the future of India more potent than that of any other man of his time, whether amongst the ranks of statesmen, warriors, or philanthropists. His father's spiritual lineage has been traced to the preaching of Charles Simeon, whose solitary sermon in a Scotch village kindled new light in the heart of the pastor whose ministry Duff's parents had long attended. The Highland farmer caught from his minister a portion of that blessed illumination, and endeavoured to communicate it to his children.

Young Duff's first introduction to missionary topics came to him through his father, who was wont to show his children pictures of Juggernaut and other heathen idols, accompanying them with explanations, which were well calculated to awaken compassion in the hearts of his young hearers for the state of the heathen. These feelings were intensified when he passed from the Grammar School at Perth, of which he had become the *dux*, to the University of St. Andrews, with £20 in his pocket, being all the patrimony that his worthy father could bestow upon his son. Here "the eagle-eyed impulsive youth" made his own way by winning scholarships and exhibitions, and had the good fortune to become at once the pupil and the friend of the illustrious Chalmers. That great man had just come to fill the chair of Moral Philosophy, and his teaching, example, and enthusiasm were like "life from the dead." He stirred the dull stagnation of moderatism into which the Church of Scotland had settled down, and won a benignant and triumphant ascendancy over the students of the university. Duff was one of that noble band of young men who came under his magic influence, and when the great Scotch orator delivered his famous prelections on missionary subjects in the Town Hall, was among the first to yield himself to the overpowering spell. Here, too, he heard Marshman and Morrison recount the story of their missionary and linguistic labours, and thus he enlarged the compass of his information, and his admiration of the work.

The missionary spirit had been awakened in Scotland: Inglis and Chalmers had infused new life into the then almost effete instrumentality called "the Scottish Missionary Society." India was chosen as the field of its operations, and the distinctive feature of this new aggression upon its heathenism consisted in the determination to call in the aid of European science, and of English literature to dislodge the absurdities of the ancient superstitions, and to reach the lead-ing classes of Hindustan, who, up to this time, had remained almost untouched and uninfluenced by Christian truth. It was no part, however, of the system conceived by these gifted men that Christianity was to be divorced from science, but rather that the latter, in all its departments, should be permeated by the influence of the former. From them " Duff imbibed his firm and noble belief in the inseparable unity of truth, and his immovable conviction that all true science pointed the way to revealed theology."

It was not, however, until he had been a third time pressed by his superiors to undertake an office, from which, (on account of his high estimate of its dignity, and his unfeigned consciousness of personal unworthiness,) he had shrunk again and again, that young Duff surrendered himself to the manifest guidings of Providence, and consented to go forth, in the strength of the Lord, to carry out the projects of his gifted teachers. All he asked was freedom from local control in India, and perfect liberty to use his own judgment as to the system of discipline and tuition to be employed in the seminary which he was commissioned to found.

In October 1829, the young missionary sailed for Hindustan, in the *Lady Holland,* with the passport of an "interloper"; so necessary, alas! in those days of intolerance. He had already won literary and scientific distinctions, as well as theological honours. To a robust frame, which had been inured to exercise and peril among his native mountains, he added that sturdy and yet cautious spirit which so generally distinguishes his countrymen, and that genial affection and vigorous intellect which, in their combination, are always so powerful and so attractive. Above all, he was gifted with fervent piety, and filled with the spirit of Divine love—his best equipment for the glorious work which he had to perform.

He was literally cast like a seaweed upon the shores of India. He had been already shipwrecked at "the Cape," and had lost his valuable library. The only thing saved from the wreck was a Bible and Psalter, which had been given him as a parting gift at his ordination, and in the preservation of which the devoted missionary read an intimation that henceforth the Book of Books must be his supreme and absorbing study. "They are gone," said he, speaking of his eight hundred volumes, "and blessed be God, I can say 'gone' without a murmur. So perish all earthly things: the treasure that is laid up in heaven alone is unassailable." He was often heard to say that this event exercised a most important influence on the whole of his subsequent career. Scarcely had the *Moira*, in which he left the Cape, entered the Hoogly, than the south-west monsoon struck her in its fury, and drove her as a shattered wreck upon the shore. The missionary and his wife were barely rescued from the rolling billows, and they spent their first night in India within the shelter of a heathen temple. Even this was a favourable introduction. "Surely," exclaimed the natives, "this man is a favourite of the gods!"

Though kindly welcomed by such men as Corrie, and Browne, and Adam, he found

that the whole missionary body in Calcutta,
with the one solitary exception of the aged
Carey, were decidedly hostile to his plans.
And we can scarcely wonder at it, for in
many cases the natives who had hitherto
come into contact with English science and
literature had turned it to bad account.
Tom Paine and his " Age of Reason " had
become the favourite author of those who
had learned English.　In the Hindu College,
where western science had been for some
time taught, but taught apart from religion,
several young Brahmins had indeed renounced
their superstitions, but were lapsing into utter
infidelity.　The missionaries saw the dangers
which were likely to accrue ; but they did not
see, like Duff, that those dangers must be
met and conquered, nor did they perceive,
like him, that new forces were at hand which
would facilitate the task.　It was in the face
of the highest authorities, in the face of
Government enactments, and of learned dis-
sertations, and despite the practice of Christian philanthropists, that Duff resolved, after
mature consideration, to repudiate Sanscrit,

Persian, and other Oriental tongues, and openly and fearlessly to proclaim English as the most effective medium of Indian enlightenment; to make it in fact what Greek and Latin had been to the Renaissance and at the Reformation, and to employ science in connexion with Christianity as the means of influencing those who, by their attainments and occupations, were destined to direct the national heart and intellect of Hindustan.

In one thing only did the bold young missionary disregard home orders; and in this act of disobedience he exhibited something of the same genius which was displayed by Nelson at St. Vincent, when he placed the telescope to his sightless eye, and refused to see the signal which would have robbed his fleet and his country of a glorious victory. The authorities in Scotland, following in the track of Bishop Middleton and of the Baptists, had resolved that the new seminary should not be established in Calcutta. Duff saw that its location there was absolutely necessary to its success; so he planted his college in the great Chitpore Road, the very centre of native life; and the issue proved that he was right.

It was opened on the 12th July, 1830. A remarkable man was present. This was none other than Rammohun Roy, the Indian Reformer, who was now approaching the close of his memorable career. At the early age of sixteen he had been led, through the study of Sanscrit and Arabic, to renounce heathenism. Having entered the service of the British Government, he had conducted himself with conspicuous integrity; but at the age of fifty he resigned his office, and entered upon a course of philosophic inquiry, which led eventually to his institution of "the Brahmo Somaj," the main principle of which was to proclaim and to practise the worship of the one supreme and eternal God. This man, though he never recognized the divinity or atonement of our Lord Jesus Christ, had conceived the deepest reverence for His teaching, and the young missionary, with quick discernment, saw how the Deistic Reformer could be rendered helpful to his own Christian plans. He therefore entered into communication with him, explained the objects he had in view, won his co-operation, and through his influence secured a number of pupils for his seminary.

Duff's biographer has given us a graphic account of the opening day. The missionary slowly repeated the Lord's prayer in Bengali. Rammohun Roy stood up to show his reverence, and the pupils followed his example. " Then came the more critical act. Himself putting a copy of the Gospels into their hands, the missionary requested some of the older pupils to read. There was a murmuring amongst the Brahmins who were among them, and this found voice in the protest of a leader: ' This is the Christian Shaster ; we are not Christians ; how then can we read it ? It may make us Christians, and our friends will drive us out of caste ! ' Now was the time for Rammohun Roy, who explained to his young countrymen that they were mistaken. ' Christians,' said he, 'like Dr. Wilson, have studied the Hindu Shasters, and you know

that he has not become a Hindu.   I myself
have read all the Koran again and again,
and has that made me a Mussulman?   Nay,
I have studied the whole Bible, and you
know I am not a Christian.   Read and
judge for yourselves.   Not compulsion, but
enlightened persuasion, which you may
resist if you choose, constitutes you yourselves judges of the contents of the book.'
Most of the remonstrants seemed satisfied."

The first and chief difficulty having been
thus surmounted, Duff threw himself with
all his native enthusiasm into his work, training his own assistants, and taking his full
share in the drudgery of the most elementary
teaching.   The institution grew in popularity; the applications for admission were
so numerous that selections had to be made.
From a school it soon developed into a
college, attended by natives of every caste,
from the Brahmin downwards, and of every
age, from eight to one-and-twenty.   At the
end of twelve months a public examination
was held under the presidency of Arch-
deacon Corrie.   Lord William Bentinck and

Sir Charles Trevelyan were amongst the audience, and expressed their surprise at the knowledge of English grammar and idiom exhibited by the boys, and still more at the ease and accuracy with which they read the Holy Scriptures, and answered questions not merely on its history, but also upon its doctrines and morals. The Governor-General afterwards, in his farewell address, described it as "a model missionary effort which even in its early years had produced unparalleled results." Visitors from distant provinces came to the Assembly's celebrated academy, caught the spirit of its plan, and returning to their own districts laid there the foundations of similar institutions.

All this was not achieved without a prolonged conflict between the Anglicans and the Orientalists; there were giants on both sides; but eventually the former triumphed. Macauley, Trevelyan, Bird, and Colvin took the same side as Duff; and when at length Lord William Bentinck, one of the greatest of our Indian proconsuls, issued the famous decree of the 7th of March, 1835, which ordained that the Government should for the future promote to the utmost European literature and science, the whole weight of English rule was thrown into a movement which must inevitably lead to the disintegration of Hinduism. The simple facts of geography, and the true theory of solar and lunar eclipses, as taught in the school, were enough in themselves to strike a fatal blow at Hindu theology ; and when the first Brahmin consented to dissect a human body in the medical college (and this was a fruit of the education received in Dr. Duff's seminary), it was felt that the system of caste had received a deadly wound.

But Duff, wiser than the British Government, kept up an intimate link between secular and religious instruction. Lectures on natural and revealed religion were publicly delivered by the young missionary, and these led to such earnest and animated debates, that the Governor-General had to satisfy himself that no political danger was to be apprehended from them. " The Hindu college" sent its ablest representatives to uphold the tottering fabric of their faith; but the controversy ended in some of the most prominent of them becoming Christians. One of these, Krishnu Mohun Banerjea, a distinguished Koolin Brahmin, became one of the most leading clergymen in Calcutta; and another, Gopeenath Nundy, was willing to lay down his life, during the Indian mutiny, as a martyr for Christ. To aid his children in the faith, the devoted missionary opened Sunday and week-day classes for the study of the Scriptures and for prayer. He erected a wicker-work chapel for preaching in the vernacular, and held an English service every Lord's Day evening. For inquirers he conducted courses of lectures on the Bible and philosophy; and when his opponents, foiled in this arena, betook themselves to writing in the Bengali newspapers, this undaunted advocate for Christian truth followed them, and made each fresh assault the occasion of a new and blessed victory.

To tell of the labours of Duff on behalf of

natives, Eurasians, and Europeans, during his first four eventful years in India, would be to write a volume, and not to sketch an outline. He soon converted the solitude of his own kirk into a goodly congregation, and his energy and enthusiasm infused such new life amongst churchmen, that the British chaplain found the attendance at his service steadily increasing. Sunday observance was at its lowest ebb when Duff came to the rescue, and restored some degree of sacredness to the day of rest. His influence was felt everywhere as that of a master-mind, as well as that of a devoted Christian.

But exhaustion was induced by all this incessant toil, and he had to return to England in 1834. What a trial to him this enforced absence proved itself we may judge from his own language when describing the spirit in which he consecrated himself to the work: "Having set my hand to the plough, my resolution was peremptorily taken, the Lord helping me, never to look back any more, and never to make a half-hearted work of it.

Having chosen missionary labour in India, I gave myself up wholly to it in the destination of my own mind. I united or wedded myself to it in a covenant, the bonds of which should be severed only by death." And so, when the great missionary left the scene of his labours, it was only to stir up the spirit of his fellow-Christians at home by such appeals as they had seldom heard before, and to give the Church at large such views of duty and of responsibility in respect to the heathen world as it had never hitherto realized. It is not too much to say that he served the cause of missions quite as much, during his five years' residence in Great Britain, as he had already done by his four years of incessant labour in India. He developed, during this period, a wondrous power of natural oratory; and those who listened to his sublime and stirring appeals came away, not like the auditors of Cicero, saying, " What a mighty orator! " but like those of Demosthenes, when they exclaimed, " Let us go and fight the enemy! " One result of these vigorous and impassioned addresses was that Scottish Christians took up the missionary work with a generous enthusiasm, and they stand distinguished to this day, above other communities, by sending out their best and ablest men to the missionary field.

His health was restored, and in 1839 he turned his face once more to the land of his adoption. But before he left he bequeathed to his countrymen a volume, under the title of "India and Indian Missions," which helped to keep alive the deep impression made by his utterances, and gave a full and graphic exposition of the superstitions and philosophies of the East. Visiting Egypt and Sinai on his way, and bringing the ardour of a boy, and the endurance of a man, to back the culture of a genial student, he wrote home charming and instructive letters concerning the desert and "the mysterious land." There are few things in the language more touching, or more sublime, than the account which he wrote from the "Top of Mount Sinai" of the impressions made on his mind by the solemn scene, while he recited on its hoary summit, upon a Sabbath day, the Ten Commandments of the eternal God. Having visited successively the missions at Bombay and Madras, and strengthened the hands of his brethren in their work, he found himself once more in Calcutta. The first object which caught his eye was in itself a token of progress; it was a sign-board, on which were marked in large characters the words "Ram Lochun Sen and Co., Surgeons and Druggists." "Not six years had passed," observes his biographer, "since the pseudo-orientalists had declared that no Hindu would be found to study even the rudiments of the healing art through anatomy." After passing the medical college, the next strange and gratifying object which met his eye was a handsome church, with Gothic tower and buttresses, and close beside it a commodious parsonage. And who was the pastor? One of his own pupils, formerly a Brahmin of the highest caste, next an educated infidel, then a humble student of the Word of Life, and now a clergyman of the Church of England, duly ordained by the Bishop of Calcutta. The large-hearted and catholic spirit of Duff rejoiced in this, no less than it did in the wonderful progress of his own institution in Cornwallis Square; and what a change did he behold as he visited his once lowly school, and thought of its condition ten years before.

"Then," he writes, "the precise line of operations to be adopted was not only unknown, but seemed for a while incapable of being discovered, as it stretched away amid the thickening conflict of contending difficulties; now there stood before me a visible pledge and token that one grand line of operation had been ascertained, and cleared of innumerable obstacles, and persevered in with a steadfastness of march which looked most promisingly towards the destined goal. Then I had no commission but either to hire a room for educational purposes at a low rent, or to erect a bungalow at a cost not exceeding £30 or £40; now there stood before me a plain and substantial, yet elegant structure, which cost between £5,000 and £6,000. Then it was a matter of painful and delicate uncertainty whether any respectable native would attend for the sake of being initiated into a compound course of literary, scientific, and Christian instruction; now six hundred or seven hundred pursuing such a course were ready to hail me with welcome congratulation. Then the most advanced pupils could only manage to spell English words of two syllables, without comprehending their meaning; now the surviving remnant of that class were prepared to stand an examination in English literature, science, and Christian theology, which might reflect credit on many who have studied seven or eight years at one of our Scottish colleges. Then the whole scheme was not merely ridiculed as chimerical by the worldly-minded, but as unmissionary, if not unchristian, in its principles and tendencies by the pious conductors of other evangelizing measures; now the missionaries of all denominations resident in Calcutta not only approve of the scope, design, and texture of the scheme, but have for several years been strenuously, and not unsuccessfully, attempting to imitate it to the utmost extent of the means at their disposal."

Dr. Duff might have spent the rest of his career in tending and expanding the institution which he had founded, but the "Disruption" of 1843 brought with it new duties, and almost a recommencement of his labours. He had held himself apart, both at home and in India, from the controversy which preceded this cataclysm; but when the announcement reached him that the "Free Church" of Scotland had sprung into life, he took his side without a moment's hesitation, and, together with his colleagues, conscientiously proclaimed himself a member of that body. This led, of course, to the surrender of the premises and the entire reconstruction of his work. But the energy of Duff was equal to the emergency, and the effect of the disruption was to double the efficiency of the mission. A new church was immediately built at a cost of £5,000. On the very night before it was to have

been opened for Divine service it fell. Undismayed, the congregation, under the
guidance of their pastor, erected another at
a cost of £12,000, and Bishop Cotton pronounced it the prettiest church in Calcutta.
Suitable and extensive buildings for educational work soon sprang into existence, and
Duff's second college is now well known in
the city as the " Free Church Missionary
Institution."

Conversions and baptisms continued, and,
as a consequence, hostilities began. Duff's
house was besieged ; he was cited into the
courts to try and compel him to the surrender
of one of his Christian pupils. The cry of
" Hinduism in danger " was raised, and this
not only, as at an earlier stage, by aristo-
cratic Brahmins, but by Mulliks and Seels,
who had risen from poverty to wealth, and
who now called in the Jesuits to found a rival
college where English would be taught *on
purely secular lines!* Duff's life was threatened;
and then he addressed a fearless letter to
the Baboos of Calcutta, in which he not only
pleaded for toleration and liberty, but

pointed out that persecution would only serve the cause which they hoped to destroy.   The closing sentences of that appeal are worth recording :—

" In the early ages of relentless persecution by the emissaries of pagan Rome, it passed into a proverb that 'the blood of the martyrs became the seed of the Church.'   Let the Calcutta Baboos rest assured that the vital principle involved in this proverb has lost nothing of its intrinsic efficacy or subduing power.   The first drop of missionary blood that is violently shed, in the peaceful cause of Indian evangelization, will prove a prolific seed in the outspreading garden of the Indo-Christian Church.   And the first actual missionary martyrdom that shall be encountered in this heavenly cause may do more, under the over-ruling providence of God, to precipitate the inevitable doom of Hinduism, and speed on the chariot of Gospel triumph, than would the establishment of a thousand additional Christian schools, or the delivery of ten thousand additional Christian addresses, throughout the towns of this mighty empire."

Duff lived down the opposition, and not only continued his great work of Christianized Education, but threw himself into various efforts for the public good. Now he is editor of the *Calcutta Review*, and spreading light by means of its pages throughout the land; now he is establishing the first hospital in Calcutta, an effort which has since expanded into ten kindred institutions; now he is aiding the Eurasians, and consolidating the Doveton Colleges of Calcutta and Madras; now he is blowing a trumpet-blast that brings relief to the famine-stricken Highlanders of his own beloved Scotland.

In 1849 there was a strong desire expressed at home that he should be invited to occupy the chair of Divinity, which had been vacated by the death of Chalmers. The bare idea of losing him created an intense sensation in Calcutta. Addresses poured in upon him, not only from European and native Christians, but from Brahmins and Pundits, entreating him not to leave them. He bowed to their request, and resolved to continue in India; but his shattered health obliged him, in 1850, to revisit his native land, and thus for three years he became again the organizer and financier of missionary work at home—stirring up the General Assembly of the Free Church (of which he had been elected Moderator) by a series of addresses which compare favourably with the highest achievements of Christian oratory; visiting England, to create amongst all classes a true appreciation of the great interests which were involved in the approaching renewal of the East India Company's Charter; appealing to the young men of London, from the platform of Exeter Hall, to come "to the help of the Lord against the mighty;" and sending out new missionaries to extend and consolidate the work which he had begun in India.

It was during this period that he appeared before the committees of the Houses of Parliament, often encountering the keen opposition of hostile questioners, but giving such irrefragable evidence as mainly led to the famous Educational Despatch of 1854. Indeed, his "handiwork can be traced, not only in the definite orders there conveyed, but in the very style of what has ever since been pronounced the great educational charter of the people of India." Well had it been for Hindustan if the principles of that despatch had been fully and faithfully carried out. Duff, when he returned to India, endeavoured to secure fair play for it, and so long as his strong hand was at the helm he was successful; but in his dying hours what grieved him most was the departure of local governments from its liberal and self-developing arrangements, and the growing inclination of "the powers that be" to give a high English education without religion; a policy which, to use his own expressive language before the Lords, was at once "blind and suicidal," and the sad results of which we are already reaping in the growing atheism of young Bengal.

Before returning, for the third and last time, to India, he visited America, and received a perfect ovation wherever he appeared. It is said that when he delivered one of his marvellous orations in New York, the vast audience was melted into tears by his pathos,

and afterwards sprang to their feet in the
wildness of their excitement. The reporters
laid down their pens; they might as well
have endeavoured to report a thunderstorm;
and when the crowds upon the wharf waved
their last farewells to him, they cried aloud,
" No such man has visited us since the days
of Whitfield."

He reached India just in time to encounter
the mutiny of 1857, and was a tower of
strength to the Christian Church in that
fearful crisis. His letters written on the
spot, and all aglow with the thrilling
emotions of the period, are a marvel of
powerful description, calm statesmanship,
and Christian heroism. The Church in India
was indeed baptized with blood, but that
fiery trial proved how deep and sincere were
the convictions of the native Christians; and
Duff, while he mourned over martyr-pupils,
could thank God for their faithfulness even
unto death.

When the University of Calcutta was
founded in 1863, the vice-chancellorship was
refused by Sir Charles Trevelyan, in order

that he might recommend Duff to that important post. His learning and his labours on behalf of education eminently entitled him to this position ; but just then his old enemy, dysentery, laid him low, and a voice from home announced that Dr. Tweedie, the convener of missions, was dead, and that Duff was wanted at home "to save the missions." It was with a sad heart the missionary took his last farewell. There is something deeply pathetic in his parting address to the Bethune Society, representing as it did all the educated non-Christians of Bengal: " Wherever I wander, wherever I roam ; wherever I labour, wherever I rest, my heart will be still in India. So long as I am in this tabernacle of clay I shall never cease, if permitted by a gracious Providence, to labour for the good of India; my latest breath will be spent in imploring blessings on India and its people. And when at last this frail mortal body is consigned to the silent tomb, while I myself think that the only befitting epitaph for my tombstone would be, ' Here lies Alexander

Duff, by nature and practice a sinful guilty creature, but saved by grace, through faith in the blood and righteousness of his Lord and Saviour Jesus Christ ; ' were it by others thought desirable that any addition should be made to this sentence, I would reckon it my highest earthly honour, should I be deemed worthy of appropriating the grandly generous words, already suggested by the exuberant kindness of one of my oldest native friends, in some such form as follows: ' By profession, a missionary ; by his life and labours, the true and constant friend of India.' Pardon my weakness ; nature is overcome ; the gush of feeling is beyond control ; amid tears of sadness I must now bid you all a solemn farewell."

He was spared, like Hezekiah, for another fifteen years, and they were not idle ones. He filled the chair of Divinity in the New College of Edinburgh ; he was chosen to the unique honour of being a second time Moderator of the General Assembly ; he inaugurated new missions in India, Africa, and the East ; he was the peacemaker wherever his voice could be heard; and at the patriarchal age of seventy-two, having "served his own generation according to the will of God, he fell on sleep" on the 12th February, 1878, full of days and full of honour.

A missionary, and much more than a missionary, Duff was a greater power in India than any of its statesmen. Their rule and influence were generally limited to some five or six years, and new men succeeded them, very often with different views of policy, and consequently with enfeebled because intermittent power; but from the time he landed at Calcutta in 1830, until he finally left it in 1864, he was an enduring and continually operating force.

His own view of his work and of its effects may be summed up in the following pregnant sentences:—"As far as education, in its most comprehensive sense, is concerned, the whole energy of my life has been devoted to the attempt to have it impregnated throughout all its departments, whether of literature, science, or philosophy, with the living spirit of Christianity. . . . And even though, in the vast majority of cases, no actual conversion ensues, good unspeakable has been gained by multitudes, and seeds have been profusely sown, which, when India is visited by the long-expected and long-prayed-for showers of grace, will spring up with a sudden and glorious harvest."

This estimate has been corroborated by one who, perhaps, with the exception of Duff himself, has done more for India, in this department of Christian labour, than any of its benefactors.

"It was the special glory of Alexander Duff," says Bishop Cotton, " that arriving here in the midst of a great intellectual movement of a completely atheistic character, he at once resolved to make that character Christian. When the new generation of Bengalees, and too many, alas! of their European friends and teachers, were talking of Christianity as an obsolete superstition, soon to be burnt up in the pyre on which the creeds of the Brahmin, the Buddhist, and the Mohammedan were already perishing, Alexander Duff suddenly burst upon the scene, with his unhesitating faith, his indomitable energy, his varied erudition, and his never-failing stream of fervid eloquence, to teach them that the Gospel was not dead or sleeping, not the ally of ignorance and error, not ashamed or unable to vindicate its claim to universal reverence; but that then, as always, the Gospel of Christ was marching forward in the van of civilization, and that the Church of Christ was still 'the light of the world.' The effect of his fearless stand against the arrogance of infidelity has lasted to this day; and whether the number he has baptized be small or great (some there are among them whom we all know and honour), it is quite certain that the work which he did in India can never be undone, unless we, whom he leaves behind, are faithless to his example."

> "Rest from thy labour, rest,
> Soul of the just set free!
> Blest be thy memory, and blest
> Thy bright example be.

" Faith, perseverance, zeal,
   Language of light and power,
Love, prompt to act and quick to feel
   Mark'd thee till life's last hour.

" Now toil and conflict o'er,
   Go take with saints thy place !
But go as each has gone before,
   A sinner saved by grace."

XI.

"God has taken away the greatest man of his generation;" so wrote Florence Nightingale, the gentlest and best of women, when she heard of the death of the great missionary explorer. "Of his character," writes a great statesman (than whom no one had fuller or better opportunities of judging), "it is difficult for those who knew him intimately to speak without appearance of exaggeration." A mourning nation has gone a good way towards endorsing these verdicts, and has given his last remains a sepulture amongst her kings. His fame was so world-wide that other countries seemed to understand him even better than his own, and not to love him less. To omit the name of such a man from these brief sketches of missionary heroes would be impossible; and yet the vastness and variety of his work, and the fact that concerning him so much has been written, and so recently, render it a difficult task. We must content ourselves with glancing at the more important features of a life and character which most of our readers have already studied in detail.

Like Duff, he was a Scotchman, and sprang from the ranks of the people. It is well known how at ten years of age he earned his bread, and helped to support the family, as a "piecer" in the cotton works of Blantyre, and how he contrived, during the long day's toil in the factory, to place his book on the spinning-jenny, and to pursue his studies amidst the roar of the machinery. His first week's wages were devoted to the purchase of the "Latin Rudiments," and he spent his evenings, and often a portion of his nights, in acquiring that language. "He could play and rollick," says his father-in-law, "like other boys, but with a growing thirst for knowledge." Books of travel and of science were his delight; and when a rare half-holiday came round, he was sure to be off to the quarries to collect geological specimens, or away by the hedgerows to gather herbs and flowers; for he had early formed the opinion that a good herbalist had in his hands the panacea for all bodily diseases.

He was religiously brought up; and he tells us, with that quiet humour which never deserted him, that his last flogging was received for refusing to read Wilberforce's "Practical Christianity." It is plain, however, that the pious example of his parents, in a poor but happy home, was his best instruction, and laid the foundation for that eminently practical Christianity which he so thoroughly understood and so fully exemplified. It was at the age of twenty, however, that the crisis of his spiritual history took place; and he attributes it chiefly to the reading of Dicks' "Philosophy of a Future State." From that time his whole heart was given to God. There is a touching entry in his journal, written upon the last birthday but one of his eventful life, and it reveals at once the motive and the earnestness of his whole career: "My Jesus, my King, my Life, my All, I again dedicate my whole self to Thee."

He had heard of missions from his childhood, and had always been deeply interested in them; but it was an appeal on behalf of China, issued by the famous Dr. Gutzlaff, which inspired him with the desire to become himself a missionary. "The claims of so many millions of his fellow-creatures, and the complaints of the want of qualified men to undertake the task,"—these, as he informs us, were the motives which led him, at the age of twenty-one, to the high resolve; and henceforth his "efforts were constantly directed towards that object without any fluctuation." The idea of medical missions was then comparatively new; but Livingstone felt that, more especially in connection with work for God in China, they were indispensable, so he resolved to qualify himself to the utmost; and by saving something out of his summer earnings at the mill, he was able to pay for his medical and Greek classes at Glasgow University during the winter, and at the same time to attend lectures in theology.

"The land of Sinim," however, was not the field which the great Head of the Church had designed for him. Just as Morrison, who had set his heart upon Africa, was led by an all-wise Providence to fill a sphere more suited to him in China, so Livingstone, whose earliest predilections were for China, was led by the same gracious hand to give his life to Africa, and to find there the very position for which both nature and grace had so eminently qualified him. He had offered himself to the London Missionary Society, and was well-nigh rejected on account of his hesitating manner and lack of ready speech. Fortunately for the world, the adverse deci sion was suspended, and another session brought out his noble character and vast capacities. But his prospect of going to China was interrupted by the Opium War, and just at this juncture a veteran mis- sionary (who would have found a promi- nent niche in these sketches, only that they are confined to the deeds of departed worthies) appeared upon the scene, and determined the destination of the student. This was Robert Moffat, who, after three-and-twenty years of labour in South Africa, was thrilling the heart of England with the story of his labours and adventures. He fired the soul of his young countryman with a desire to explore and evangelize that mysterious land, with which both of their names will ever be identified. Indeed, it has been well said that if any heroes of modern times might be permitted to adopt the grand old agnomen of "Africanus," Robert Moffat and David Livingstone, who soon became his fellow-labourer and son-in-law, would be the men.

We are indebted to Professor Blackie for a biography of our hero, which gives the world a deeper insight into his inner and social life than could be obtained from his own official journals. These latter are generally marked by that characteristic reticence which caused him to conceal from the public gaze all that was best and noblest in his nature. It is only from his private letters, to his nearest

and dearest ones, that we get the full por-
traiture of a man who was as gentle as he
was resolute, and as loving as he was strong.
The account of his last evening in the old
homestead is touching in its simplicity: "A
single night was all that he could spend with
his family; and they had so much to speak
of, that David proposed they should sit
up all night. This, however, his mother
would not hear of. 'I remember my father
and him,' writes his sister, 'talking over the
prospects of Christian missions. They agreed
that the time would come, when rich men
and great men would think it an honour to
support whole stations of missionaries, instead
of spending their money on hounds and
horses. On the morning of the 17th November, 1840, we got up at five o'clock. My
mother made coffee. David read the 121st
and 135th Psalms and prayed. My father and
he walked to Glasgow to catch the Liverpool
steamer.' On the *Broomielaw*, father and
son looked for the last time on each other's
faces. The old man walked slowly back to
Blantyre, with a lonely heart no doubt, yet

praising God. David's face was now set in earnest toward the dark Continent."

His first nine years in Africa were spent chiefly amongst the Bechuanas, nine hundred miles from Cape Town. Here, with unwearied earnestness, he laboured for the evangelization of these uncivilized and rude barbarians. Here, too, he endeavoured to instruct them in useful arts; and, after the example of mediæval missionaries, he laboured as a mechanic no less than as a preacher. At Kolobeng we find him helping to make a canal, preparing a garden, and building his fourth house with his own hands. Moffat had taught him how to work in iron and steel, while at the same time he became expert in carpentry and other trades. His devoted wife (Mary Moffat) made the butter, soap, candles, and clothes, instructed her infant-school, and taught the women to sing the hymns which her husband had translated. They had their privations and trials, and often lived "from hand to mouth;" but theirs was in the truest sense a happy life. As he reviews this part of his

African career, he finds but one cause of regret, namely, that he did not devote more time to playing with his children; "but," he adds, "I was generally so exhausted by the mental and manual labour of the day that in the evening there was no fun left in me." How touching are the lines which in after years, when he was separated from his family, were ever ringing in his ears,—

"I shall look into your faces, and listen to what you say,
  And be often very near you when you think I'm far
    away."

It was during this period he had that famous encounter with the lion, which is known to nearly all who have heard his name; but concerning which he wrote home thus characteristically to his father; "I hope I shall not forget His mercy. . . . Do not mention this to any one. I do not like to be talked about." Livingstone's life was saved almost by a miracle, but the left arm, which was crunched by the lion's teeth, was maimed for life, and the fracture entailed much pain and suffering to his latest days. It is well known that it was by the false joint in that broken limb that his body was identified, when brought home to England by his faithful followers; but the interesting fact is not generally known that Mebalwe, who saved his life, was one of the native teachers whom he himself had trained, and that it was a Christian lady in Scotland who contributed the money for this catechist's maintenance. How little did she dream that the twelve pounds, which she had sent to Livingstone for that purpose, would be the means of preserving to Africa for thirty years the life of its greatest benefactor!

The firstfruits of Livingstone's missionary labour in this region was the conversion of Sechele, a chieftain of extraordinary energy, who was soon able to read the Bible in his own language, and to conduct his own family worship. Sechele, transformed in feelings, dress, and manners, used all his influence to induce his people to follow his example, but without much success. Livingstone, however, had laid a good foundation, as the results have proved. "That mission," says Dr. Moffat, writing in 1874, " is the most prosperous, extensive, and influential of all our missions in the Bechuana country."

Livingstone now entered upon the special career which has made his name so famous, namely, that of a missionary explorer. Many considerations led him to the conscientious belief that this was the path peculiarly assigned to him by Providence. The oppressions practised by the Boers of the Cashan Mountains upon the Bakwains first awakened his attention to the evils of the slave trade, and he longed to see it crushed out by Christianity and lawful traffic. He conceived it to be the duty of the missionary, when he had fully published the Gospel to any people, to press forward and make it known to those who had never heard it. His heart yearned over the countless millions who must be living in the interior of that vast unexplored continent, and who had never yet been visited by the messenger of peace. He felt, moreover, that God had given him peculiar talents for this work, and that it was his duty to employ them in the way most likely to advance the great cause which he had at heart. Writing to a friend at this time, he tells him about " the tsetse, the fever, the north wind, and other African notabilia" ; but these and many other interesting points of information are followed up by the significant question, " Who shall penetrate through Africa ? "

Livingstone himself was to be the answer to this question ; and he offered himself and all that was dearest to him—home, prospects, honours, Christian intercourse—as a willing sacrifice upon the missionary altar. It would be a great mistake to think that the mere love of exploration and adventure, or even the fame that might possibly accrue from them, were sufficient to influence a mind like his. When he had achieved his greatest reputation as a discoverer, he expressed the honest feeling of his heart, in reminding those who had conferred distinctions upon him, that "where the geographical feat ends, there the missionary work begins."

We can only summarize the story of those

wonderful journeyings, which revealed to us, for the first time, the teeming populations and boundless resources of Central Africa. Previous to his time the charts of this vast region presented nothing but a blank. To use the quaint words of Dean Swift—

> " Geographers in Afric's maps
> Put savage beasts to fill up gaps,
> And o'er inhabitable downs
> Put elephants for want of towns."

What a change, and what a revelation! What bright hopes and prospects for commerce, civilization, and Christianity, have sprung up in that benighted land since the dauntless explorer unlocked the door, and opened it wide to the traveller, the merchant, and the missionary!

The natives had often spoken to him of a lake which they called Ngami; and in June, 1849, he set out, with Messrs. Oswald and Murray, with the hope of discovering it. Skirting by the great Kalahari desert, he pursued his way, and on the 1st of August had the satisfaction of being the first white man to see that now famous lake. Finding

that region insalubrious, he undertook (in
the year 1850) another expedition.   On this
occasion he carried his wife and children
with him to the Makololo country, where he
made what was perhaps the most fruitful of
all his discoveries—that of the great river
Zambesi, flowing in the very centre of the
continent, with its majestic reaches and its
" smoke-resounding "   falls.   His   eyes
gladdened as he gazed upon this unexpected
highway for future commerce ; for he saw in
it a providential aid towards the extinction of
that accursed traffic in human flesh and blood,
which met him everywhere, and which made
his very heart to bleed.

But what was to be the outlet for that
commerce, and how was he to obtain the best
and shortest route to the coast ?   These were
questions which forced themselves upon his
consideration ; for the southern Boers had
invaded the Bechuana country, pillaged his
old settlement at Kolobeng, and broken up
the organization which had cost him so many
years of labour.   His resolution was prompt
and decisive.   He carried his family back to

Capetown (where it was observed that his coat was eleven years behind the fashion), despatched them to England, and then started on that arduous journey which led him from Linyanti, in the very centre of Africa, to Loando St. Paul, on its western shores. He found, however, that that port was too distant, and too difficult for convenient access, and that it was moreover too nearly connected with the slave trade to answer his purpose.; so he retraced his steps, and travelled right across the vast continent to the mouths of the Zambesi on the eastern coast.

This perilous journey occupied four years, and never did a body of men voluntarily set out on such a serious undertaking with so spare an outfit. For himself and his twenty-seven black companions the stock of provisions consisted of a few biscuits, a few pounds of tea and sugar, and about twenty pounds of coffee. The supply of clothing was equally scanty, and the money-chest contained only twenty pounds of beads, worth about forty shillings. Three muskets for his people, with a rifle and double-barrelled smooth-bore for himself, were all the firearms which the intrepid traveller took with him, although on these and on their ammunition mainly depended their supplies of food. " I had a secret conviction," observes Livingstone, "that if I did not succeed, it would not be for the lack of nicknacks, but from want of ' pluck,' or because a large array of baggage excited the cupidity of the tribes through whose country we wished to pass." His tact and his fearlessness carried him safely through many a danger amidst hostile tribes, whilst his justice, and his kindliness, and his truth endeared him to his swarthy followers. The latter always spoke of him as their " Father," while many of the former came to regard him as a god. He was ready at any moment to endure any sacrifice, or to brave any danger, if only he could save a life, or soothe a sorrowing heart. A messenger arrived one night, and told how a native had been attacked by a rhinoceros, and ripped open. Livingstone, in order to relieve the wounded sufferer, started immediately, and forced his way for ten miles through tangled brake and thicket, amidst the midnight darkness, despite the risk of a like fate awaiting himself at any moment. Such was his philanthropy; but better and nobler still was that love of souls which led him evermore to make known to all men the message of redeeming love. His simple sermons, his earnest prayers, and his Sunday services marked him everywhere as "the man of God."

In 1856, preceded by the fame of his discoveries, he revisited his native land. The enthusiastic welcome and the triumphal honours that awaited him might well have spoiled a less noble spirit. But if Livingstone had his failings, the love of popularity was not one of them. He was characteristically humble. When a great man once expressed admiration at his wonderful achievements, he simply replied, "They are not wonderful; it was only what any one else could do that had the will." His one thought was for Africa—"Poor, enslaved Africa," as he was wont to say, "when are

thy bleeding wounds to be healed?"
Wherever he went he tried to deepen the
national interest on behalf of his adopted
country. To this end he appealed to the
Geographical Society with respect to its
exploration, and to our leading statesmen
with reference to the suppression of its
slave trade. He aroused the Universities
to its claims upon their intellectual powers,
and the Churches to its demands upon
their Christian charity. With the same
object in view, he sat down and wrote his
"Missionary Travels," which was a kind
of employment so distasteful to him that he
says in the preface, "I would rather cross
the African continent again than undertake
to write another book!"

He had told his faithful followers in Africa
that nothing but death would keep him from
returning to them, and he kept his word.
In 1858 he started on his second great
expedition to explore the Zambesi. On this
occasion he went forth under a Government
commission, with a regular staff of assistants, and with a small steamer called the

Ma Robert, which was Mrs. Livingstone's African name; but this expedition cost him more anxiety and pain than all his previous journeyings. Good Bishop Mackenzie, who had gone out in connection with the Universities' mission, and had joined Livingstone in his explorations, fell a victim to the climate.; several other members of the mission shared a like fate; and, saddest of all, Mrs. Livingstone, who had joined her husband, was also taken from his side, 27th April, 1862. They had been only three short months together, after four years' separation. Two days after her death he wrote to Sir Roderick Murchison: " This heavy stroke quite takes the heart out of me. . . . I married her for love, and the longer I lived with her I loved her the more. . . . I try to bend to the blow as from our heavenly Father. . . . I shall do my duty still; but it is with a darkened horizon that I set about it."

This second expedition resulted in the discovery of Lake Shirwa and Lake Nyassa, and tended materially towards the suppres-

sion of the slave trade, by revealing its
enormities, and the awful destruction of
human life which it involved at the hands
of the Arab and Portuguese traders. "I
sometimes fear," says Livingstone, "that
my statements, which are within the truth,
may be looked on as exaggerations; but
the facts cannot be overstated. We saw
three instances of bodies tied to trees, the
hands fastened behind to the tree, and a
strong thong, round the neck, to the same
tree keeps the body in a sitting posture even
after death. This is the way in which
these vile half-caste Arabs vent their spleen
when a slave is no longer able to walk—
vexed at losing their money, they secure
their death. . . . It is quite a relief to get out
of the beat of slave-dealers; they glut the
market with calico and gunpowder, and
send one tribe to plunder and destroy
another." It was thus that he gave a voice
to the silent agonies of Africa, and made
that voice to be heard throughout the
civilized world; nor, when he had the opportunity, did he hesitate to take the law into

his own hands, and to strike the fetters from the limbs of the bleeding slave.

He had shed his last bitter tears beside *Ma Robert's* grave, and was about to launch his steamer, the *Lady Nyassa*, on which he had expended £6,000 of his own money, when, owing to political and financial reasons, the expedition was recalled by our Government. He resolved to sail to India and sell his ship before he returned home. The Portuguese would have bought her, in order to use her as a slaver; "but," writes Livingstone, "I would rather see her go down to the depths of the Indian Ocean than that." His engineer left him, so he had to turn skipper himself, and to navigate his vessel from Zanzibar to Bombay, a distance of 2,500 miles, amidst alternate squalls and calms, with no other aid but that of three Europeans and seven natives, most of whom were disabled by illness during the voyage. But he reached Bombay, where he sold his ship for one-third of what she had cost him, and then sailed for England.

He did not tarry longer amid the luxuries

of home than to write his second volume,
" The Zambesi and its Tributaries." His
heart was in Africa; and when the Geographical Society proposed to him to go
out and discover the great watersheds
of Central Africa, and settle the long-
disputed question of the sources of the Nile,
he at once responded to the call; but to his
honour be it spoken, that when they wished
him to go forth " unshackled by any other
occupation," he nobly replied, " I can only
feel in the way of duty by working as a
missionary." His last public words in his
native Scotland will be long remembered as
the epitome of his own life: " Fear God and
work hard." And so he set forth in 1865
upon his third journey, not without fore-
bodings that it would prove to be his last.
" I set out on this journey," he writes,
" with a strong presentiment that I should
never finish it. The feeling did not interfere
with me in reference to my duty; but it
made me think a great deal of the future
state, and come to the conclusion that
possibly the change is not so great as we

have usually believed. The appearances of Him who is all in all to us were especially human; and the Prophet whom St. John wanted to worship had work to do, just as we have, and did it."

Taking Bombay in his way, he obtained from the missionary school at Nassik some of those young liberated slaves, whose fidelity to their master, in life and death, have won for them the admiration of the world. Eight of them volunteered for the service; and these were supplemented at Zanzibar by some Johannamen and Sepoys; the former were thieves, and the latter proved to be so intolerable that he soon dismissed them. The party dived into the depths of the unknown continent, and were lost to the cognizance of the outer world. Anxious months of expectation passed by, and no tidings concerning them arrived. At length one of the Johannamen arrived at Zanzibar, with circumstantial news that Livingstone had been murdered on the shores of Lake Nyassa. The story was only half credited in England, and the painful suspense was at length relieved in 1868 by letters from the missionary himself, telling how the Johannamen had deserted him, but how he had made the important discoveries of Lake Tanganyka and Lake Bangweolo. On May 30th, 1869, he wrote again from Ujiji; it was the last intelligence received from him up to July 1872, and it told a tale of suffering and illness, but yet of unconquerable resolution. He was without medicine or suitable food; suffering from hemorrhage, and scarcely able to walk from weakness; whilst a war that was raging near him cut off both communication and supplies; but he makes little of his deprivations, and with a touch of his old humour he writes to his daughter Agnes: " I broke my teeth tearing at maize and other hard food, and they are coming out. One front tooth is out, and I have such an awful mouth. If you expect a kiss from me, you must take it through a speaking trumpet" ; and again, "the few teeth that remain are out of line, so that my smile is that of a hippopotamus."

After this he pushed on into the Manyuema

country, with the determination of examining
the Lualaha river, and settling the question
of the watershed. All kinds of difficulties
surrounded him; massacres and atrocities
were of frequent occurrence; most of his
followers failed him; the Arab slave-dealers
bullied and thwarted him; his feet were
lacerated by hard travel, and his strength
exhausted by fever and dysentery. On one
occasion he narrowly escaped death three
times in a single day. Then we find him
confined to his hut for eighty days,
"harrowed by the wickedness he could not
stop, extracting information from the natives,
thinking about the fountains of the Nile,
trying to do some good among the people,
. . . and last, not least, studying his Bible,
which he read four times over whilst he was
in this region." Everything seemed to be
against him; no news from home or country
came to cheer him; but the brave spirit of
patient faith could not be quenched. "All,"
said he, "will turn out right at the last."
"I commit myself to the Almighty Disposer
of events, and if I fall, will do so doing my

duty, like one of His stout-hearted servants."

He returned to Ujiji, the 3rd of October, 1871, "a mere ruckle of bones," to find that his goods had been plundered, and he himself beggared in his absence. Truly he had fallen amongst thieves who had stripped him, and he was half dead; but who was to be the good Samaritan who, three days later, should unexpectedly pour oil and wine into his bleeding wounds? The story of his discovery and relief by Stanley are too well known to be repeated here. Statesmen and scientific societies in England seemed to have passed by on the other side; and to the intrepid young American belongs the honour of having preserved a little longer that invaluable life. Restored to comparative health and energy, Livingstone was entreated by his deliverer to return with him; but, though he had not seen a white man for six years, and yearned after home, he steadfastly refused. His heart was set upon solving the problem of the Nile, not so much, as he again and again assures us, for the sake of the discovery, as from the conviction that it would give weight to his pleadings on behalf of down-trodden and enslaved Africa. His impressions about the sources of the Nile were that they were far higher than any previous traveller had supposed, and in this, though he did not live to know it, he proved to be mistaken; but the great object on which he had set his heart was eventually realized. He had said in his parting lectures at Bombay, " Perhaps God in His providence will arrest the attention of the world to this hideous traffic by some unlooked-for means; " and amongst the last words he wrote were these: " I would forget all my cold, hunger, suffering, and toils, if I could be the means of putting a stop to this cursed traffic."

The end was drawing near, and his death was to be the means of awakening more attention to the subject than his life had ever done; for his last words, now deeply graven upon his tomb, became still more deeply engraven on the nation's heart: " All I can say in my solitude is, may Heaven's rich blessing come down on every one—American, English, Turk—who will help to heal this open sore of the world."

Stanley had left him, and sent up supplies and men from the coast; amongst the latter were some more pupils from the Nassik School. No sooner had they arrived than he set out once more for Tanganyika and Bangweolo. The pathway lay through deep morasses and flooded rivers, and amidst incessant rains. The natives proved un-friendly; hunger frequently assailed the party; his illness returned, and any but an iron frame would have succumbed at once; but he bore up bravely, and, as his journals prove, his faith remained unshaken. " No-thing earthly will make me give up my work in despair. I encourage myself in the Lord my God, and go forward." He pursued his investigations, but at length the strong man was utterly broken down. They had reached Ilala; and as he could go no further, his followers built a hut, and laid him beneath its shade. The next day he lay quiet, and asked a few questions. On the following morning (4th May, 1873), when his boys looked in at dawn, his candle was still burning; and Livingstone was kneeling by the bed, with his face buried in his hands upon the pillow. He was dead! and he had died upon his knees, praying, no doubt, as was his wont, for all he loved, and for that dear land to which he had devoted three-and-thirty years of his laborious life!

And that desolate band of followers whom he left behind, what a marvellous proof they gave of his influence over them, and of their deep attachment to him! They resolved to carry his remains to Zanzibar, and give them up to his countrymen; and so they embalmed the body, and reverently laid his heart, and all that could not be removed, in a Christian grave. Jacob Wainright, one of the Nassik boys, read the burial service, and carved an inscription on the mvula tree that overhung the spot. And then began such a nine months' march as the world had never witnessed, whilst these sons of Ham carried the body of their loved master to the coast; braving all risks; flinging aside all prejudices; at times fighting their way through hostile tribes; at others succeeding in carrying out their plan by stratagem, but never desisting from their labour of love until they gave up their sacred charge into the hands of the English consul. Well might they say as they surrendered their precious burden :—

" Where will ye lay the form that enshrined
  Daring so glorious and valour so kind?
  Where shall be rest for the vigorous hand,
  Hush for the brain that made weariness grand ?

" Meeter to rest 'mid the tombs of the kings,
  Ne'er shall be poet that soars as he sings ;
  Warrior that stormeth the newly-made breach,
  Martyr that suffers, or mind that may teach.

" Lay him to rest where ye will, he is *ours !*
  Strew on his hearse of Eternity's flowers.
  Bear him, O ship, from the deserts he trod ;
  Waft him, O Death, to the garden of God ! "

Livingstone had once come upon a native grave, not very far from the place where he himself was destined to die ; it was a little rounded mound, with blue beads strewn upon it, and with a little path beside it, plainly showing that it had visitors. " This is the sort of grave," he writes, " I should prefer; to lie in the still, still forest, and no hand ever to disturb my bones; ... but I have nothing to do but wait till He who is over all decides where I have to lay me down and die. Poor Mary lies on Shupanga brae, and ' beeks fornent the sun.' "

But God so ordered it, and the love and admiration of a mighty nation so desired it, that he should lie in a nobler sepulchre. And so the doors of Westminster Abbey were opened for perhaps the most striking funeral that ever crossed its threshold; and as the anthem pealed through the stately aisles, they laid him down to sleep amongst the mighty and the great, and princely hands cast wreaths of flowers upon his coffin, and men of every class and creed bowed down their heads and worshipped; and some were there who, twelve years before, had helped him to lay *Ma Robert* in her lone and distant grave; and he was there who had found the long-lost missionary, and rescued him from death; and one was there, more moved than all the rest—that swarthy son of Africa, who now helped to bear his pall, but who had nursed him gently in his sickness, and who had laid his loving heart to rest amongst the people for whom he had lived and died.

It was the first time in the history of the nation that a missionary hero was thus honoured. Shall we say that this was so because such men have usually died at their distant posts? or was it rather because we were all too slow at home to recognize their bravery and their worth? Whatever be the reason, one thing is beyond dispute, that no one ever obtained this distinguishing honour at the hands of Englishmen who was better entitled to receive it, and that the whole civilized world has endorsed their tribute of admiration.

There is a well-known journal which is the representative of our national wit and humour; but which, when it condescends to be grave, never fails of being both

touching and sublime. Within a border
of the deepest mourning it set forth the
following lines on the sad occasion; they
are worthy of their theme, and form a
suitable conclusion to this brief record of
a noble life :—

" Droop half-mast colours ; bow, bareheaded crowds,
    As this plain coffin o'er the side is slung,
To pass by woods of masts and ratlined shrouds,
    As erst by Afric's trunks, liana-hung.

" 'Tis the last mile of many thousands trod
    With failing strength, but never-failing will,
By the worn frame, now at its rest with God,
    That never rested from its fight with ill.

" Or if the ache of travel and of toil
    Would sometimes wring a short, sharp cry of pain
From agony of fever, blain, and boil,
    'Twas but to crush it down, and on again !

" He knew not that the trumpet he had blown
    Out of the darkness of that dismal land,
Had reached and roused an army of its own
    To strike the chains from the slave's fettered hand.

" Now we believe he knows, sees all is well ;
    How God had stayed his will and shaped his way,
To bring the light to those that darkling dwell
    With gains that life's devotion well repay.

" Open the Abbey doors, and bear him in
    To sleep with king and statesman, chief and sage,
The Missionary come of weaver-kin,
    But great by work that brooks no lower wage.

" He needs no epitaph to guard a name
    Which men shall prize while worthy work is known;
He lived and died for good—be this his fame:
    Let marble crumble : this is Living-stone

XII

THOSE who remember the " Eton Montem," that grandest of all school festivals, will recall the brilliancy of the annual pageant, when lords and ladies of high degree came down from London to witness the procession of enthusiastic students, as it made its boisterous way to Salt Hill, in order to collect the accustomed votive offerings for the captain of the college. Brilliant, however, as the " Montem " was at all times, that of 1838 surpassed all that went before it. Queen Victoria, who had recently ascended the throne of her ancestors, had come from her kingly residence at Windsor to grace the scene with her presence. The Eton boys were beside themselves with excitement, and crowded around the royal carriage with vociferous and tumultuous loyalty. One of them, a brave, impetuous youth of eleven years of age, became entangled in the wheels, and was on the point of being dragged under them, when, with that presence of mind which has since so often distinguished her, the youthful Queen stretched out her hand to the falling boy. He grasped it, recovered his footing, and was saved. Before, however, he could regain his self-possession, the royal *cortège* had moved on, and left him no opportunity for expressing his gratitude to his deliverer.

·Thirty-four years afterwards, the same illustrious Sovereign, when opening her Imperial Parliament, made a touching allusion to "the murder of an exemplary prelate" in the South Sea Islands, and urged upon her senators the duty of adopting measures for the suppression of that nefarious practice of labour-stealing which had led to his death. She had rescued that noble missionary bishop, when he was yet a boy, from what might have been instant death; and she mourned for him now as one of that " noble army of martyrs" who had laid down their lives for the cause of Christ in distant lands.

It was a "new thing in the earth" to hear a missionary spoken of with admiration in a royal speech; but Bishop Patteson deserved the mention, not merely on account of his heroic end, but still more on account of his heroic life.

The son of one English judge, and the nephew of another, he was born to ease, affluence, and honour, but was led to renounce them all for the work of God among the heathen. The earlier missionaries of this century, with scarcely an exception, had sprung from the lower ranks of society, but the time had come when the noble and the great were to consider themselves honoured by following in their steps. Three years had elapsed since his memorable escape, and Coley Patteson, as his comrades loved to call him, went with several other Etonians to hear Bishop Selwyn preach to his old flock at Windsor. This great missionary prelate had just been consecrated to his New Zealand see, and was infusing something of his own enthusiasm into the hearts of all who heard him. In a letter to his mother, Patteson records his impressions of the sermon: "It was beautiful when he talked of his going out to found a church, and then to die, neglected and forgotten: all the people burst out crying; he was so very much beloved by his parishioners. He spoke of his perils, and of putting his trust in God; and then, when he had finished, I think I never heard anything like the sensation; a kind of feeling that if it had not been on so sacred a spot, all would have exclaimed, 'God bless him!'"

It was not the first time that Coley Patteson had heard of missions. Nurtured in the bosom of a Christian family, he had already not only resolved to devote his own life to the ministry of the Gospel at home, but had begun to take a decided interest in the work of missions abroad. This sermon, however, and an incident which followed it, gave a new direction to his choice. Bishop Selwyn came to take leave of the Pattesons, with whom he had long been intimate, and in doing so he said to Lady Patteson, half in play and half in earnest, " Will you give me Coley? " The question startled the fond mother, and she made no reply at the time ; but when the boy told her that " the one grand wish of his heart was to go with the bishop," she replied that if that continued to be his wish when he grew up, she would give him both her consent and her blessing. Alas! she only lived a year, and did not see the fruit of that request and of that promise. But she had taught him to read his Bible at five years old, and it was that very Bible which was afterwards placed in his hands at his consecration.

No boy was more popular at Eton than Coley Patteson. He was decidedly clever, but inclined to be idle. When he chose to put forth his powers, he was successful. He was full of fun and frolic, but always distinguished for his courage and patience. Famous at cricket, he was beloved as captain of the eleven. He could handle an oar as dexterously as any one upon the river, and

he was a perfect expert in the art of swimming. He little knew how well these manly
exercises were fitting him for future service
in a higher sphere. During all his schoolboy
life he maintained a noble consistency. At
one of the annual dinners given at Slough,
by " the eleven " of cricket and " the eight "
of the boats, one of the boys began to sing
an objectionable song, and Coley instantly
called out, " If that does not stop, I shall
leave the room." This remonstrance being
unheeded, he took his departure, followed by
some others as brave as himself. Nor was
this all; he sent back word that unless an
apology were made " he would leave the
eleven," a threat which soon brought the
offender to his senses, and made his companions feel that Patteson's consistency was
not to be trifled with. He left school without " sting or stain," and his father wrote
him a letter on the occasion, in which he
attributes his son's blameless career to the
assistance of God's Holy Spirit, and to the
pious instruction which he had received from
the best of mothers.

His college life at Oxford tended to develop his character. He refused to join the eleven because he feared cricket would prove his tyrant, and he had resolved to work. He induced the young men at Balliol to give up their dessert in order to aid the sufferers in the Irish famine. He distinguished himself as a scholar, and especially as a linguist; became a fellow of Merton in 1852, and was soon remarkable as a college reformer. Too pure for party, and too steady to be moved by any gusts of false doctrine, he maintained his religious convictions unimpaired, and his attachment to his own Church unshaken, amidst surrounding agitation and defection. There was a reserve, and yet a charm in his manner; a spirit of introspection, which, as his biographer puts it, was at once his strength and his danger; a love for all things beautiful, coupled with a strong and sensible attachment to what was practical and useful. After obtaining his fellowship he spent five years in foreign travel; and Professor Max Müller, speaking of him in reference to this period, says, " I saw him last at Dresden in 1853, revelling in the treasures of ancient Italian art, working hard at Hebrew, Arabic, and German, and delighting in all that the best minds of modern Europe could supply in literature, science, and art. I then thought I saw in him the future accomplished dean or bishop; but when I heard of him next, his letters were dated ' longitude ' and ' latitude,' from some unknown island in the Pacific Ocean."

He was ordained for a charming parish, situated near his father's beautiful residence in Devonshire, and he had before him every prospect of an honourable and happy career in the midst of friends and relatives; but before a year had passed by, the Bishop of New Zealand, who had come to England to look for helpers in his work, was on a visit at Sir John Coleridge Patteson's, and the old fascination, which twelve years before had been so strong upon the boy when he heard the Bishop preach at Windsor, came back upon the young curate with a still stronger power as he walked and talked with the man who had been so long the object of his admiration. That visit and those conversations set the seal upon his determination. He opened his heart to his father, and he, "with the fullest sense of his own loss, yet with the most unhesitating heartiness, gave up one who was dearer to him than life. No father and son could be more tenderly attached; none could feel separation more sensibly; but neither wavered for an instant in his resolution." Sir John, writing to the Bishop at the time, says, " If he prove an effectual instrument in New Zealand—as I heartily pray Him he may be found—I shall feel that I have in some sort made a present of him to the work of the Lord Jesus Christ, and that it is a blessed thing to have done so." There is something exquisitely tender in the record of Patteson's departure from the parental home. The last farewells had been spoken; the last kisses had been given; the sisters watched him till he had disappeared from sight, and then returned, to find their venerable father sitting silently over his Bible.   Meanwhile the brother whom they loved so well had turned aside into the churchyard, picked a few early primroses from his mother's grave, "*and then walked on !*"   He had put his hand to the plough, and he never looked back.

He embarked with Bishop Selwyn in the spring of 1855, and reached New Zealand in July.   During the voyage he made such progress in the art of navigation, that he felt as much at home with a quadrant in his hand as of old with a cricket-bat, and acquired such facility in speaking the Maori tongue that, on his arrival, one of the senior clergy was asked the not very complimentary question, "why he did not speak like Te Patehana (Patteson)."   His own special mission was to be in the Melanesian islands, which lie near the equator, and are peopled by a race less intelligent, but more steady, than the Polynesians.   They had no elements of civilization, and scarcely any ideas of religion, through which they could be influenced.   They enjoyed a very unpleasant reputation for cannibalism, and were styled

" the irreclaimable savages." They spoke, moreover, throughout their vast archipelago, such an infinite variety of dialects, that it was humorously observed " they must have come straight from the tower of Babel, and gone on dividing their speech ever since."

He spent the first five years of his missionary life in making voyages, in company with Bishop Selwyn, amongst these islanders, and then returning to the missionary college, where their training school was held. Their plan of operation was to induce the natives to give up some of their youths for instruction, and then to bring the latter to New Zealand, where they remained under Christian teaching until the winter-time approached, when it became necessary to carry them home to their own more genial climate. The islanders soon learned to place confidence in the missionaries; and as each year brought back a number of the youths with their glowing and grateful accounts of the treatment which they had received, fresh pupils were continually offering, and many of the old ones willingly returned to complete their

Christian education. It was no uncommon thing to see the Bishop and Patteson, as they approached one of these reef-surrounded islands, take off their coats, and fastening some hatchets or other gifts upon their backs, take a good header into the surf, and swim ashore. We can picture them to ourselves as they go through the ceremony of rubbing noses with the natives by way of greeting; then the entering into friendly communication with them, and eventually departing with a precious freight of "raw material," in the shape of swarthy boys, to be worked up by means of kindly teaching into hopeful pupils, and brought back in due time to spread abroad amongst their countrymen the knowledge which they had received.

The time had now arrived when the Melanesian Mission was to be entirely surrendered to the care of Patteson, and when, in order to this, he was to be made a chief pastor. Bishop Selwyn had trained him to his work, and gives the following graphic description of his singular fitness for it: " I wish you could see him in the midst of his thirty-eight scholars at Kohimarama, with eighteen dialects buzzing round him, with a cheerful look and a cheerful word for every one, teaching A B C with as much gusto as if they were the $x\,y\,z$ of some deep problem; or marshalling a field of dark cricketers as if he were still the captain of the eleven at Eton; and when school and play are over, conducting his polyglot service in the mission chapel." His amazing power as a philologist stood him in good stead, and with a skill second only to that of Mezzo-fanti, he reduced to system and to grammar between thirty and forty of those hitherto unknown languages.

He was set apart to his high office in St. Paul's Church at Auckland, on the 24th of February, 1861. The consecration was not by royal mandate, for the Anglican Church was now beginning to extend its episcopate beyond the British dominions; but there were other incidents which gave their own pecu-liar impressiveness to the scene. Selwyn was there to lay his hands upon the head of

the beloved pupil, whose young enthusiasm
he had been the first to kindle. A Maori
deacon was there, and several native
teachers with their wives, to represent the
new-born church. Ten of the island boys
were there to witness and to rejoice in the
consecration of their revered instructor;
one of them, Tagalana, like a living lectern,
held the book from which the chief prelate
read; and the Bible which was delivered
into the hands of the new Bishop as the
symbol of his office and the guide for his
work, was the very same which had been
given him on his fifth birthday, with his
father's love and blessing. One who witnessed the ceremony observed that Patteson,
clad in his quaint rochet, "reminded her
of some young knight watching his armour,
as he stood in his calm steadfastness and
answered the questions put to him by the
Primate."

His own feelings proved him worthy of
his office. "I don't suppose," he writes,
"that I realize it yet; but I shall have to
learn what it is to be a bishop by the trials

and anxieties which will come. God will doubtless give strength if I seek it aright; but here is the point—I need the prayers of you all. . . . And now to me it is permitted to hold up the weak, heal the sick, bind up the broken, ' *bring again the outcasts, seek the lost* '—those wonderful, beautiful words. How I held tight the Bible my dear father gave me on my fifth birthday with both hands! and the bishop held it tight, too, as he gave me the charge in the name of Christ, and I saw in spirit the multitudes of Melanesia scattered as sheep amidst a thousand isles." It may be mentioned here that he had already arranged with his father that his own share of the paternal inheritance should go to his beloved mission; and on hearing what the amount of it was to be, he writes: " Hard enough you worked, my dear father, to leave your children so well off. . . . My children now dwell in two hundred islands, and will need all that I can give them. God grant that the day may come when many of them may understand these things, and rise up to call your memory blessed ! " The father lived to hear of his son's consecration, and to rejoice in it; but within four brief months from that event he was called away, and the best of sons had to mourn for the best of fathers.

To tell the story of that too brief episcopate would be to recount the perils and the labours of ten such arduous, yet happy years as have seldom fallen to the lot of man. "In perils of waters," as he navigated his *Southern Cross* from isle to isle throughout what has been happily called his "ocean see;" "in perils by the heathen," as ever and anon he landed on some coral reef in the presence of naked and armed savages; "in weariness and painfulness," as he endured the hardships and the diseases which were inseparable from a life like his; in "watchings often," as he tended his sick and swarthy pupils through the lonely nights, with all the skill of a nurse, and all the tenderness of a parent, he realized to the minds of men the ideal of an apostolic missionary, and did much to restore its true character to the much-ill-used and often merely conventional title of " Bishop."

What a sight it must have been to see him standing up in his boat as he approached some hitherto unvisited island, extending his arms to show the suspicious warriors on the shore that he carried no weapons, then plunging half-naked into the sea, and swimming to the land amidst the wonder of the awe-struck savages! The very boldness of Patteson was oftentimes his safety. Who could bend a bow or hurl a spear against a man so trustful and so brave? And when it happened, as it often did, that in their suspicion or their fear they pointed an arrow at him, it was his custom to look the archer in the face, with that bright and sunny smile which seldom failed to restore confidence, or to disarm hostility.

His principal missionary college for training youths was eventually established at Norfolk Island. It was more convenient for his work, and its more genial climate rendered unnecessary the return of the pupils, during the winter months, to their own homes. It was here that the love and the labour of the missionary prelate found their chief employ. "I am so accustomed," he writes, "to sleeping anywhere, that I take little or no account of thirty, forty, fifty naked fellows, lying, sitting, sleeping around me. Some one brings me a native mat, some one else a bit of yam; a third brings a cocoa-nut; so I get my supper, put down the mat (like a very thin door mat) on the earth, roll up my coat for a pillow, and make a very good night of it." He was never so happy as amongst his boys or his books; and the former were so fond of him that they would steal into his humble study of ten feet square, just for the pleasure of being near him, and of getting now and then a gentle word or a loving smile. He threw himself, with all his old Etonian enthusiasm, into their games and sports; he tried to make them all as joyous as himself; he loved to hear their merry uproar when he started them upon a race, or sent up for them a fire-balloon.

How his heart yearned over them as he taught them the way to heaven, and saw in one or another the first strivings of the Spirit of God; how lovingly and anxiously he fanned the first sparks of spiritual life in their hearts, and how wisely and gently he dealt with all their religious difficulties; how gladly he admitted them, with more than a father's love, to the sacred font, and yet how cautious he was not to prostitute the sacrament of baptism into an idle form: " I can't baptize people morally good, who don't know the name into which they are baptized. . . . To say the word, 'I believe,' without a notion of what they believe, surely that won't do. They must be taught, and then baptized according to our Lord's command, suited for adults."

His sorest trials were connected with the death of some of the boys whom he loved so well. What a proof it was of mutual affection when one of them said with his dying breath, " Kiss me, Bishop." But there was not merely the pain of parting from them, and the loss which the mission sustained by their removal; there was also the difficulty of breaking the sad news to their heathen parents, and the danger of incurring the ignorant resentment of the islanders, and thus preventing fresh supplies of pupils.   On one occasion a boy died at the college, and he belonged to an island the language of which Patteson had not yet fully mastered.   What was he to do? Would he avoid that island in his next voyage, or would he go there, and run the risk of not being able to exculpate himself? He determined on the latter course.   He landed on the island, sought out the father of the boy, and took him by the hand.   The tribe gathered inquiringly around, and watched and listened, as partly by words and partly by gestures the Bishop began to tell his tale.   He described the lad's illness, and taking a child that stood near, laid him gently on the ground, and hung over him, and kissed him to express his love.   Then the Bishop gasped for breath, and closed his eyes, to show the progress and issue of the disease ; and then he wept over the child as it lay before him, to show them how he felt when the boy was dead.

Never was the progress of a drama watched with such intense interest as that. When it came to the crisis of the child's death, the warriors grasped their weapons; but when they looked on the white man's face, and beheld his undissembled tears, they believed him, and felt that he was their friend:—"It is all well, Bishop; he died well. You did all you could, Bishop; it is all well."

No marvel that the work of such a man should be successful. At the end of 1870, he could report that at Norfolk Island there were 180 Melanesians, of whom 62 had been baptized, and 12 more were preparing for that ordinance. These youths proved their sincerity by voluntarily proposing to go to other islands, where the dialect was like their own, and to undertake missionary work. In 1871, the *Southern Cross* brought back twenty-nine native Christians to settle in their own homes, and at the end of that year there were more than 300 Christians living amongst their own friends, and diffusing amongst them the blessed truths which they had themselves received. They were representatives of nearly all the islands that stretch from the "New Hebrides" to the "Solomon Group," and cover nine degrees of latitude. One of the most remarkable of Patteson's boys was George Sarawia. He belonged to Vanua Lava, one of the Banks' Islands, and, while yet a child, had scrambled of his own accord into the Bishop's boat. He was the first Melanesian admitted to holy orders (1868), and was stationed by the Bishop on the island of Mota. In that infant church this native pastor baptized 293 persons, and carried on beside a most successful work in the neighbouring islands.

But we must come to the terrible tragedy which took away the head of the mission to his great reward. About the year 1869, the demand for labourers in Queensland and Fiji had led the captains of trading vessels to cajole the natives of the Melanesian islands on board their ships, and then, thrusting them under the hatches, to carry them off to the distant scene of their enforced labour. In several instances, terrible reprisals had been inflicted by the natives upon English crews for this nefarious conduct. Again and again pathetic appeals were made to the Bishop to try and get them back their friends who had been thus stolen away, and again' and again he had appealed to the authorities to put down this horrible traffic. But still it went on, and, infamous to relate, Patteson's influence with the islanders • was fraudulently employed to push the abominable trade. Sometimes the captains of these "kill-kill" vessels, as the natives called them, would pretend that, as he could not come himself, he had sent their ships to fetch the islanders; sometimes they would paint them to resemble the *Southern Cross;* and there is reason to believe that on some occasions the sailors dressed up on deck a clerical figure with book in hand, to represent the Bishop, in order to inveigle the unsuspecting natives on board. Deeds like these had awakened apprehensions, both at home

and in the mission, for the Bishop's safety;
and the sequel proved that they were not
unfounded.

It was on the 20th September, 1871, that
the missionary schooner stood off the island
of Nekapu, not far from Santa Cruz. The
Bishop had frequently landed here before,
and it was only in the previous year that
he had been kindly welcomed by the inhabitants. Some canoes lay off the island,
but the people did not come out to meet
him as on previous occasions, and this
was looked upon as strange; but the good
Bishop, fearing nothing, got into a boat with
Mr. Aitken and three native Christian
youths, and pushed off through the blue
waters for the coral strand. On reaching
the reef, it was found that the tide was
too low to allow of the boat crossing it; so
the Bishop got into one of the canoes, along
with two chiefs who had been always friendly
to him. The boat's crew could not follow,
but they saw the Bishop land, and then he
was lost to sight.

Suddenly a man stood up in one of the

canoes, and shot an arrow into the boat, crying out, " Have you anything like this?" A shower of arrows followed from the other canoes, and before the boat's crew could pull her out of range, three of them had been wounded, two of them, as it afterwards proved, mortally. They made the best of their way to the ship, and when the tide began to rise, sent back the boat in search of the Bishop. The boatmen crossed the reef, and saw the canoe drifting towards them. As they neared it, a yell of triumph rose from the shore. The boat came alongside, and two words passed from lip to lip—" The body ! " There it lay, beneath a native mat, but stripped of its clothing. The face bore no trace of agony, but wore its own sweet smile of love. There were five wounds—no more ; and the frond of a cocoa-nut palm was fastened on the lifeless breast, with five knots on the long green leaves. It was all unconsciously that his murderers had adopted for him the emblem of Christian victory ; but it was not difficult to discover the meaning which they had themselves attached to their symbol. Five men had been lately stolen from Nekapu, and the untutored savages had taken vengeance upon the first white man who fell into their hands; probably with the full belief, for reasons already alluded to, that he was accessory to the wrong.

It is remarkable that not long before, in his appeal to the Provincial Synod of New Zealand, this noble-minded Bishop had said: "I desire to protest by anticipation against any punishment being inflicted on the natives of these islands who may cut off vessels or kill boats' crews, until it is clearly shown that these are not done in the way of retribution for outrages first committed by white men. . . . It is not difficult to find an answer to the question, 'Who is the savage and who is the heathen man?'"

Alas! that one of the noblest of missionaries should be the victim of the treachery and deceit practised, by his own countrymen, upon people for whom he would willingly have laid down his life. This consolation remains—his death called public attention to the evils which were the cause of it, and his work survived him. Several of those whom he evangelized are now ordained as Christian ministers; the truth of the Gospel has won its way amongst the people for whom he lived and died; and another Selwyn, son of that missionary prelate who enlisted Patteson in the Melanesian field, has succeeded the martyred Bishop in the government of the Melanesian Church.

And so we close our sketches of modern missionary heroes with the record of one who was second to none of them in the lofty bravery of Christian faith, or the grand devotedness of Christian love. " To have known such a man," writes Max Müller, " is one of life's greatest blessings. In his life of purity, unselfishness, devotion to man, and faith in a higher world, those who have eyes to see may read the best, the most real *Imitatio Christi*. In his death, following so closely on his prayer for the forgiveness of his enemies—' for they know not what they do '—we have witnessed once more a truly Christlike death."

How will ye mourn the warrior, that fell as warrior ought?
How praise the hero that hath found the glorious meed he
　　sought?
Ah! drop no tear upon the page that burns beneath his
　　name—
Breathe never sigh, but raise your song to notes of proud
　　acclaim!

How shall we name thee?—as a Knight of ancient line
　　and true,
That kept his Knighthood's vigils, and all its training
　　knew,
That look'd on all the world could give, and scorn'd its
　　ease like dross,
To bear the foremost banner in the Battle of the Cross?

How shall we think of thee?—as one who dared the winds
　　and waves,
On Heaven's sublime discovery, and brake men's living
　　graves;
Whose mighty mind in patience turn'd its wide linguistic
　　lore
To wake the first Te Deum on a Melanesian shore?

Ah! no, thy style and title owns a bearing far more bright,
For MARTYR is a grander name than hero, sage, or
　　knight.
The lofty joy was thine, afar upon the wilds to trace
The Master's life! and loftiest souls wear still the lowliest
　　grace.

*　　*　　*　　*　　*

An oarless boat is floating within the wide lagoon—
It holds a strange, dark, silent mass, that ye will know too
  soon.
No soul is there, and from the lips there comes no voice
  of prayer.
Row, row beneath the Southern Cross, with the burden
  ye must bear ;

And lay your Bishop on the deck, and look your last, nor
  weep—
There will be time enough for tears when ye give him to
  the deep.
Smooth out the blood-stained vestment's fold, with the
  reverent touch of love,
And think upon the Crown of Thorns that won our crown
  above !

Leave him in rest ! no hope forlorn was that his Saviour
  led,
Whose love is deeper than the sea that shrouds His
  sainted dead ;
Whose mysteries of grace sublime transcend time's little
  loss,
And all our pain, with all our sin, we lay beneath His Cross.

Yet mourn ye must ; but mourn as those who look'd on
  Stephen's smile,
And closed the eyes that saw the Lord beyond death's
  awful aisle.
Rouse ! by that vision, rouse ! for love and shame of heart,
  to pray
That He who gifted such a soul would quicken ours
  to-day.

O Crowns of all the martyrs ! O Lives of all the saints !
O Choir of Christ's redeemèd hosts ! your noblest anthem
    faints,
Your bravest light but sparkles dim before the glory due
To Him who bought you with His blood, and gave HIM-
    SELF for you ! *

* These lines, as well as those upon Livingstone at page 310, are
from the pen of Mrs. Alessie Faussett.

Hazell, Watson, and Viney, Printers, London and Aylesbury.